Indulgences, Discipline and Consequences

RILEY BEDWYN

Contents

Party Foul

The house was huge, and so was the party. Kevin seemed oblivious to his family's wealth, but Alex quickly felt lost in the rambling mansion.

The football game of the year was on that night, and among Kevin's friends and numerous cousins were fans of two teams. They would want to watch one game in real time and the other Tivo'd.

It was going to be a long night. Alex didn't care at all for football, but she needed a good time, and through the deepening haze of boredom that made up her relationship with Kevin these days, she grasped at the chance.

She scanned the basement, a gigantic Man Cave affair with numerous doors leading to stairs climbing up to the second, then third floor, and others to the wine and beer cellars. She could dimly hear people above them, watching on the other big-screen TVs.

She was out of place and felt it keenly. There were only two other girls there that she could see, both wearing team jerseys. Likely sisters or cousins. Alex preferred a more femme look and always took care with her appearance. For tonight, she'd chosen textured tights, booties, and a snug little skirt balanced by a soft, drapey sweater with a lace bralette underneath. Her hair was a loose tumble of curls, and dewy makeup finished it all.

Kevin forgot her almost immediately. She watched him disappear into a knot of fist bumps and bro-hugs and thought, Fuck this.

She could sulk and be dramatic, but what was the point? Alex straightened her spine and tossed her hair. She'd make her own good time. First, a drink. She made her way up to the main kitchen.

There, she met Terry. She noticed him juicing a lemon into some crushed ice to mix with gin. Terry was shy at first, but he made her laugh, and his smile was real. He was slim and Black, with a soft fuzz of beard and eyelashes to make a cosmetic model sick. His long locks were held back with a scarf so yellow it was almost blinding. As they talked, Alex learned that he was a nursing student invited along by his brother and didn't know Kevin.

Even while Alex listened to what he was saying, she couldn't help but let her eyes wander. She liked the way Terry's fingers moved, as if they each had their own brain and he barely needed to concentrate on them. He'd make an excellent nurse, Alex already knew. Maybe he'd be a surgeon one day. Then her thoughts really did wander. Terry in soft green scrubs, washing those nimble hands carefully, his hair twisted up out of the way. It was unexpectedly erotic. A tiny ache curled somewhere inside her, as deep as the bottom of the well.

Soon, their conversation lowered in volume but deepened in meaning. They adopted a conspiratorial posture, bent toward each other on their elbows over the kitchen island. Terry's eyes were wandering over her too, Alex realized. They were close enough that their breath misted the air on their faces. The question was asked and answered. Alex went upstairs first, and three minutes later Terry met her there. They found an unoccupied hallway and began to devour each other.

His mouth tasted of lemons and felt like pure sin. The soft hair on his jaw brushing her cheek made her scalp tingle. His hands molded to her body instantly, as if he'd known her for a hundred years. Terry's fingers dug into the back of her thigh and hip. He kneaded the flesh of her ass. His voice in her ear was low and urgent. She nodded eagerly as he went to his knees. She pulled up her skirt for him.

Terry's tongue was all heat, sliding into her as soon as her panties were out of the way. He pulled one of the legs of her tights all the way off, along with her shoe. Alex heard the nylon rip but didn't care. She placed one foot on the opposite wall and gave herself up to him.

He planted kisses in a wandering journey up her inner thighs. She quivered as he sucked on the sensitive skin. His breath was even hotter than it had been on her face. Alex squirmed, ready to beg, but was finally rewarded when he grasped both her hips and dove in.

A moan tore itself from her throat as his mouth covered her needy cunt. Alex slapped a hand over her mouth. She couldn't stand the thought of being deprived of his touch before she had taken all she could. He kissed her lower lips fervently, overloading her senses and making her thighs shake. Her voice rose again as he sucked on the tender flesh of her hood, dancing on the edge of Too Much. She whined against her palm.

She was about to tell him to ease up when he slowed, and the words died. For a moment, all she felt was his hot breath. His tongue made a leisurely circuit, paying court to her outer lips, dipping inside them to start another circle a little smaller than the first. The sensation grew as he steadily spiraled inward, over and over, around and around.

When he reached her entrance, he thrust his tongue into her. Alex moaned and whined, feeling him take direction from the noises she made, fucking her with his tongue again, flattening it against her upper wall. She placed one hand against the side of his head, resting it there, barely feeling the texture of the brilliant yellow scarf. The other she brought up under her sweater. The hard bud of her nipple was against the lace of her bralette, almost scratching. She pinched one of them between her small fingers and let out a small yelp. Terry groaned at the sound. His tongue worked at her entrance for several long, wonderful minutes. It wasn't quite long enough to reach the swollen spot inside her that would break it all apart. She wanted it so badly yet not yet, not yet. Alex ground her hips against his face and was rewarded with a deep but gentle kiss to her clit.

The depths inside her began to rise, growing to a slow boil. Terry spread his lips into an O and sucked gently. When that drew a low hum, he laid his tongue just under that spot and continued the sweet torture.

Alex knew then that she was fully under his power, that he could ask anything of her at that moment and she would gladly agree just so he wouldn't stop.

As her mind rose away from her body into thin air, liquid fire poured through her from all directions at once, vaporizing her consciousness as she came against his mouth, around his tongue. Her cunt flexed, making the waves crash even harder through every neuron and synapse. She could feel her walls closing around his tongue again and again, trying to pull it deeper into herself, to possess it.

As her mind slowly came back down into her body, she was dimly aware of Terry kissing her inner thighs again. When she remembered what sight was again, Alex looked down. He knelt before her, wiping her juices from his lips and sucking them off his fingers. She didn't know if she'd ever seen anything more erotic in her life.

"Don't move," Terry said. "I'm not done." He reached up quickly and took Alex by the hips. He spun her around, her feet shushing against the carpet, and moved his hands to grasp a double handful of her ass.

Alex only had time to make a small "Oh!" sound before Terry's tongue covered her asshole. He flicked it, tickling her, then wiggled the tip of his tongue into her pucker and began to move it around. It felt like a tiny, wet finger playing with the sensitive skin. He squeezed her buttocks hard, making them shake. Alex closed her eyes and groaned softly. She was slick from her mound to the top of her crack. She reached back and tapped Terry on the shoulder that she'd had enough. For a moment, she only stood there with her ass pushed out.

She pulled her panties up and slid down the wall slowly to face him, a tangle of stockings, damp curls, and a drunken smile.

"Your turn. Lean against the wall." Terry got up. Her hands were already working at his belt buckle, yanking at the zipper.

Alex wrapped her fingers around his cock. Slowly, she stroked up and down the shaft, keeping her grip gentle, then rubbed the head against her lips. He was so hard, like silk over marble. He smelled good, like clean clothes, a hint of something that might have been coconut oil, and his own body chemistry.

She dipped her head and started to make a line with small, wet kisses up the underside and the fine ridge that lived there. When she reached the head, she stopped to circle it with her tongue before sucking just the glans in, ever so gently, between her lips, pressing the flat of her tongue on the underside. Then she pulled away to kiss and lick down the side. She went back up to the head again, and down the other side. His breath caught in his chest.

Alex took in a long breath through her nose as she took him into her mouth, working herself down with swirls of her tongue until he slid freely between her lips. She locked her fingers snugly around the base of his cock and began to bob her head. Her lips made a tight seal, and her tongue ran lasciviously anywhere it could reach.

Terry's hand came down to frame the side of her face, her jaw, and wandered up to bury itself in her hair. It tightened. His thumb brushed over her cheek, feeling how it bulged around him. She felt how tense his muscles were, how he vibrated in her hands, her mouth. He was struggling not to push her head down and his cock down her throat, she knew.

She looked up as best she could in time to see his eyes start to roll back in his head. She sucked harder and got a sharp intake of breath. His hand let go of her hair and reached down to touch her shoulder.

"I won't..." he panted, "Do it in your mouth if you don't want..." Alex grabbed him by the hips and held him firmly, gagging herself a little, rubbing the head of his cock against the back of her throat. That pulled him over the edge. He stuffed a hand over his mouth as he shuddered, sending rope after rope of hot jism down her throat. Alex flattened her tongue and worked her throat to gulp it down, pulling it straight from his balls. She felt them pulse under her fingers. They leaned against each other for a moment, just existing.

After they parted, Alex went to the nearest bathroom and stared at herself in the mirror. She almost expected to see CHEATER written in bright red across her face, but she didn't look guilty. She looked... good. Her eyes shone and her lips were flushed, the gloss all kissed away. Her tights went straight into the wastebasket. She glanced at the shower – she could take another few minutes for a rinse. Alex slid off her clothes.

The evidence of her pleasure was subtle above the waist. Her nipples were a little flushed, that was all. But her entire pelvic area shouted out her pleasure. Alex leaned against the wall and admired herself. Her lower lips were plump and dark pink. The creases of her thighs were shining with feminine arousal. She turned around and stuck her ass out to see what Terry saw.

The door opened. Alex yelped and snatched for a towel.

"Oh, fuck! Sorry!" the man said, putting a hand over his face. Alex tilted her head to get a better look at him. "Derek?"

"Alex?"

Derek was an ex-friend's ex-boyfriend who had represented their school in a few swim competitions. He was tall and toned, with pretty gray eyes and a perpetual case of mild sunburn on his Irish skin. His shorts always rode low, exposing his prominent hip bones. Alex liked that.

Derek went to leave but Alex stopped him. He obeyed, but slowly, unsure of himself. He didn't want to admit it, but she pressed him coyly until he confessed that he felt a little heated over the cheerleaders, hadn't had much company since the breakup, and had come looking for a private spot to relieve some tension. Alex looked down at his crotch and could see that he was still on his way to an erection.

Alex looked him in the eyes and let the towel slip away from her body. She needed relief too, she told him.

"That's why I came here," she said, and slid her hands down to caress herself. It didn't take much persuading after that to get him into the shower.

Derek's hands moved over her body as if he had to map it all out in a matter of seconds. His palms molded to her, flaring his fingers open moving up her ribcage, squeezing her ass like Terry had, trailing his fingertips gently across her collarbone, making her shiver. She wanted to climb him like a tree.

Her nerves sparked when Derek's tongue swirled over her nipples and down to the undersides of her breasts to trace their swell against her body. Every suck and lick made her clit pulse, still sensitive. His mouth traveled up from her breasts to play over her clavicle. When that drew a sigh, he placed his hands on either side of her head and tilted her chin up. Derek leaned down and kissed her throat.

"Ohhh," Alex moaned. He'd gone straight to one of her sensitive spots without indication. His tongue made slow circles around her voice box. She could feel herself getting wet again, from inside, while he laid small kisses just under her chin. Mist from the shower washed over her vision.

The warm water coursed over her skin, and his hands flowed over her curves like a fast river. She didn't want to wait any more. Derek's cock was at full mast and twitching with need when she took him in her fingers. She placed a hand around his cock and cupped his balls with the other. Alex stroked the tender skin. Derek had his back to the spray. It was obvious that the fat drop of clear fluid that leaked from the tip of his cock down his shaft was not water.

He had to have her, he panted. "Please."

"Yes! Yes, NOW," Alex demanded.

Derek's hands went to the backs of her thighs. He lifted her up against the wall, ankles crossed behind him, locking them in place. Alex braced her arms around his shoulders and felt him press his hard length against her.

His mouth was against her ear, voice almost hoarse. He made her beg to be fucked as he slid his shaft up and down between her lips, taking obvious satisfaction in the sound of her need. Her cries and pleas grew lower in volume but higher in pitch as she was pushed to the point of dizziness.

When he finally pressed the tip into her, she could make no sound. He eased himself in slowly, inch by inch, into her wet heat. Her body offered no resistance at all. He slid her down on his cock slowly until their bodies were fully joined.

Derek buried his face in her breasts, filling his mouth with her smooth flesh. He began to move inside her, outside of her, move her all over. Her back slid against the tile, his tongue swept over her clavicle, his teeth worried at her nipples.

His hip bones dug into the flesh of her thighs as he thrust more firmly. Alex rolled in a sea of bliss, the moans in her throat moving lower. Derek fucked her a little harder, never picking up too much speed at once. He was making this last, she knew. He had no intention of putting her down until she made him or until he was done with her.

Alex's ears pounded with the sound of her own pulse and the sounds coming from her seemed to be coming from someone else. It wasn't quite enough to get her there, but it was more than enough to drive her mad. She clawed at his back, clenched her thighs around his waist, meeting his thrusts with her own.

The way he shivered, his body breaking out in gooseflesh despite the warmth of the water, told its own story. He groaned in eager pain as her nails scored his skin, and latched his mouth onto the spot just under her jaw, sucking, nipping, and licking. She was sure to have all kinds of marks the next day.

No language was enough to convey the need tearing through her like a forest fire. Derek let her suffer for several awful wonderful minutes until he gave her relief. Alex's mouth opened in a soundless wail as her nerves blazed. She felt her cunt clamping down on him over and over and reminded her arms to stay strong so she wouldn't slip.

Three thrusts later, Derek pulled out with a sound like agony. His cock slid over her ass as he came against the shower wall. To his credit, he let her down well if a little awkwardly. They dried off and dressed quickly, knowing they had both been gone too long already, and joined a few others on a second-floor balcony.

Derek produced a few joints, and the party improved. People came and went, including Derek, with a smile and his phone number. Kevin even showed up. He had indeed been looking for his girlfriend, but was far from concerned or annoyed.

"You look so sexy tonight," he whispered in her ear, his breath smelling of warm beer and chips. Alex's stomach lurched. Kevin was honestly beginning to disgust her. She resolved to start planning the breakup. She pasted an empty-headed smile on her face and cooed thanks at him. Kevin pressed himself up against her back with an arm around her waist. Alex put Kevin out of her mind and concentrated on his body, without an identity. She ground her ass against the crotch of his jeans, small movements, just enough to let him feel it. He exhaled against the back of her neck.

"When we get home, I am going to fuck you good and hard," he slurred. He'd had a few more beers than she thought, Alex realized. He might not be able to get it up. She put on her cute voice anyway.

"Mm, oh yeah?" she teased. Kevin replied by sliding a hand down her back and grabbing her ass hard. He lowered his hand further and began fumbling at the hem of her skirt.

"Why don't we just slip away and…" She had to stop him. She twisted around in his grasp to face him.

"But this is your party, and you're the host."

"So?" he returned. "I –" Alex put a finger to his lips.

"Shh-shh. Soon, baby. Soon," she promised. She looked at him with her sultriest face, challenging him. It worked. He looked down and nodded.

"All right. But you're getting it good and hard later."

She felt the smirk in her mind when she pecked him on the lips, knowing he wouldn't pick out the smell or taste of two other men on her. Then he too was gone. For a moment, Alex was alone, watching the last rays of light disappear into the pines. The cool breeze made her nipples stiffen. As much as she'd already done this night, still her current ran high, urging her on. More. We want more.

"Alex." This time it was not a question. Alex felt her jaw drop when she turned to see another person she knew – knew rather well, though they had only dated two months. Tomás was an exchange student from Spain, now back in town after graduation.

In seconds, it was like they had never parted. His big brown eyes drew her in and he smelled exactly the way he had before, of books and coffee with sugar. He wanted her at least as much as she wanted him. She could see it in his face. His eyes shone. In a few more seconds, they had escaped into a nearby guest bedroom.

The lock clicked tight behind them. No one had ever kissed her like Tomás had. He could make her drunk in approximately two seconds. She tasted whiskey in his kiss. The thing about Tomás was that he was both a teaser and a pleaser. Every bedroom encounter with him was a true adventure.

He turned her around and ran one hand under her sweater. His hand was sure of itself. It pushed up her bralette and claimed her breasts, one and then the other, playing with her nipples, feeling her shapes. Tomás's mouth found her neck as he pushed down her skirt to squeeze her behind with his other hand.

"You know how I wanted this ass," he breathed. I've been thinking about it ever since I last saw you, and how you used to tease me with it. I know you remember too."

She did remember. She had wanted to try anal with him, but circumstances cut them off, and he had to leave the country before exploring her ass. She had had anal sex a couple times since with others and wasn't impressed, though she didn't hate it either. She knew Kevin wanted it. He would try sliding his cock between her cheeks sometimes when he spooned her and had even prodded at her with his fingers a few times until she shooed him away. Alex had begrudgingly let him lick her ass once but made sure to lie still and quiet so he would give up. This was different. She didn't care if it would hurt. She needed to feel his cock in her ass. Even the guest bedrooms had ensuite bathrooms, and this one yielded a small tub of Vaseline. He turned her again to face the mirror.

"You're going to watch yourself get fucked in the ass." Just the sound of him saying that made Alex moan. Tomás held her tight against him with one arm as he had before, kissing her like it was the last time he ever would. His other hand pressed the cool jelly against her asshole. It felt deliciously dirty and a little ticklish as he swirled his finger. It was like a little tongue, nudging unapologetically against her hole, begging sweetly to be let in. Was it supposed to feel this good? It had felt good when Terry licked her asshole, but this was almost obscene.

"Hey. I said watch," his voice came. She had indeed had her eyes closed. Alex opened her eyes and looked at her reflection. She'd seen herself after Terry had pleasured her, but it was a whole new look when she was about to get fucked. A look of anticipation and need that almost looked like fear. Her eyes were dilated and her lips were parted. Her hands gripped the countertop. She still had her sweater on, but could see her skirt down around her knees, trapping her legs.

Alex could see Tomás behind her, his eyes on her ass. One hand rested on the small of her back, making her present. She trembled and felt her asshole give a little spasm on its own, opening around his fingertip as if pulling him inside. Slowly, far too slowly, he worked his finger into her, then back, then in again. Tomás pushed his finger all the way into her ass and twisted it slowly, then moved it around in circles, stroking the inside of her ass. Alex reached behind her and spread herself in a plea for more. He only continued with one finger.

"Please," she said in a small voice. He didn't react. Alex knew he was pretending. "Please," she said.

"What do you want me to do?" he asked. "Say it exactly."

"Please, another finger. Or your cock. I don't care, I need more."

He added a second finger, and stars burst behind her eyes. The Vaseline had melted and was wonderfully slick as his fingers entered, still as slowly as ever. Alex rose up on her toes without meaning to, and Tomás's hand on her back pushed her town. It made his fingers thrust into her ass a little harder. A little cry came from her throat.

"Quiet," he ordered, but his voice was almost a purr.

Her clit was on fire from her mound pressed against the countertop, and his fingers stroked pleasure points deep inside her. She didn't know if he went on for a few seconds or many minutes. Alex groaned aloud and felt him chuckle. She realized with a blush that he hadn't moved his hand for a minute. She had been unconsciously fucking herself on his fingers.

Alex made a sound of disappointment when his fingers vanished. She looked behind her. Tomás was opening his pants. Alex's cunt pulsed when she saw his cock again. She had missed it more than she knew. He coated his cock in Vaseline and rubbed the tip against her in slow circles, waiting for the pleasure to be enough for her hole to open for him. He was harder than marble. When he entered her, she let out a small gasp at the feeling of giving way. Her ass cheeks quivered around his cock as he stood motionless, only the tip gripped by her anus, squeezing him. The sensation of not being able to close her asshole always took her a minute to get used to. The outer ring of muscle stung a little from being stretched in a way it hadn't been for... she didn't know how long. She wanted this, she just had to persuade her body to want it too.

Another breath, and he slid in another inch. Her ass immediately clamped down again. "Here," he said, and put her hands on his hips. "You're in control." She moved him slowly, minutely, bit by bit, all the way inside.

She could feel the soft curls at the base of his cock tickling her crack. She had never been so full. When she released him, he was still.

"Fuck me," she breathed.

He began to make the tiniest movements, back and forth. He was not thrusting inside her, but rubbing her with his cock, massaging her insides, working her open. Alex placed her fingers on either side of her pussy lips, spreading her fingers in a Y-shape, closing her lips on each other to caress her sensitive clit with flesh softer, slicker than any tongue. The sensations joined to create something new, hot, fierce.

She looked up to see Tomás's face with pleasure written all over it. Mouth slack, eyes half open and upturned, breath coming in soft, urgent puffs. His hands moved up to travel over her body, over and under her clothes, every inch that he could reach. A steady stream of English mixed with that sexy Castilian dialect tripped from his lips. She remembered how much she loved watching him shatter. It was rising in her too. Her hand over her pussy moved faster.

The spasms took her. Her head fell forward, mouth open. She felt herself pulsing around him, and he was done for. He shivered against her, grasping her hips hard as he came in her ass. Alex felt his balls warm against her vulva. He ground himself in to the root. Tomás stayed inside her until he went soft, then slid his cock out of her ass. He went to his knees. She felt his tongue again, soothing her aching hole. It slipped into her hole. She felt her fucked-open anus opening and closing around him. Alex didn't know she could be more turned on knowing he could taste his own ejaculate. Tomás straightened up.

"Don't wash just yet. Keep it inside you for a while." His thumb made circles around her asshole. It was slippery with Vaseline and semen, but she jumped a little at the contact to her sensitive flesh.

They could barely stand to separate, but she knew she'd see him again soon. The mirror showed her a woman who had definitely just gotten fucked. She hadn't even stood up straight yet. Her hands gripped the countertop still, and her skirt and panties were still around her knees. There was some pain, but it was good.

Alex dressed again and checked her reflection in the mirror. Her clothes still looked all right, but her curls were coming down and her eyeshadow had creased. She patted the bit of rose gold shimmer back into place with her finger and made her way out to the bedroom. Her legs were wobbly. Time to go downstairs for food and drink. The door to another room opened and closed.

"I knew it," a male voice came from behind her. Alex whirled around to see Jordan, Kevin's best friend. His face was pale, his blue eyes hard.

Jordan was in the university orchestra. She had noticed him when Kevin stopped to talk with them once on the way across the quad. She'd made up an excuse to go to the next performance and was quickly aroused when she saw how he dragged his bow across the cello, making it moan and sing. Jordan looked good in a suit, wearing it as easily as if it were pajamas, with strands of his long blonde hair escaping the band at the nape of his neck.

Alex had crossed her legs in her seat, making her dress ride up her thighs, and tightened herself again and again, nearly reaching climax. That night, she had ridden Kevin hard, bouncing on his cock in the dark while she thought of Jordan. Now, Jordan's face looked a bit like it had on the stage— intent. Focused. She hadn't been able to see his eyes very well from her seat, but now they were two chips of ice.

"You fucked him, didn't you?" he prodded. Fear stabbed her in the chest. She willed indignance to take its place. Her words finally came.

"Don't try to get in my business, Jordan." She made to walk past him but his hand flashed out and grabbed her arm.

"Don't even think about it," he warned. There was something dangerous in his voice that forced her to obey.

Jordan yanked Alex sideways toward the bed. She saw him descend, then the world swung wildly. She gasped – this couldn't be happening. Guys didn't just put women over their knees anymore, only in old movies and porn. But she was here now, ass up, hands spread on the floor.

"I've been thinking you were fucking around on Kevin for a while now." Her legs wiggled as he pulled down her skirt. The stretchy material moved easily. It felt like the tenth time that night that someone had pulled her skirt down.

"Jordan, don't –" He cut her off.

"And now I'm going to find out if I'm right." She felt her panties yanked down her legs. Her eyes squeezed shut, and she hung her head. She'd done her best to clean up quickly, but she knew what Jordan saw – the deep pink of her full, soft pussy lips. The smell of cum and female arousal on her. Her hot pink, slightly distended asshole, still shiny with Vaseline. She'd done as Tomás said and kept his cum inside her. She heard Jordan breathe in.

"You have. Another man's cum. Leaking out of your asshole." His voice was cold fury. Then everything happened at once. His hand grabbed her hair and wrapped it around his fist, pulling her head up. Her mouth opened but his hand struck her first, crack! Then she couldn't have made a sound if she'd wanted to.

Stinging blows rained down on her backside faster than she could count. Her feet swam uselessly in the air, toes tapping the floor. Her skirt was around her calves. She would not be able to run away even if she could get up. Her panties were rolled tightly against her thighs.

He went on as if he intended to spank her forever. Each impact was a shock to her system, both the force and the sting of skin against skin. It felt like being lashed with a thorn branch. She could hear music, muffled voices, could hear the party going on as she lay over Jordan's lap, getting her bottom blistered by his big, experienced hand.

He was saying things, things about her being a trifling little cunt with no loyalty, that he couldn't believe she'd have the gall to cheat on Kevin in his family's house, but all of this barely touched her ears. Each strike hurt, but she was once again desperately turned on. Any nerve that hadn't been activated before now flared to life. Her clit rolled against his leg every time they moved. The pain made her clench her ass, sore from being fucked by Tomás only minutes ago. Was he ever going to stop?

A steady whine began in her throat. Jordan growled at her to shut up, but she couldn't help it. Any moment she would lose control and start wailing. If she did that, someone would surely hear. He seemed to sense this and slowed, dealing broad open-handed smacks to her ass, making it jiggle. Somehow that hurt worse.

"Jordan... stop... I'm sorry..." she sobbed. The blows slowed. After several more, they ceased. His fingers slid between her legs to find the new wetness there.

"Disgusting," he whispered. "Like a little bitch in heat." Alex's head spun as she was pulled off of his lap, bent over, and pushed onto the bed. Jordan took hold of her skirt and panties and pulled them off her hard. She heard a few stitches give way. His hands grabbed her by the ankles and shoved her legs apart. She was fully exposed to the fingers that returned to her vulva. His pointer finger slipped into her slit. She moaned and arched against his hand.

"Hmph. Maybe if you're good, I won't tell Kevin."

She felt him climb up onto the bed, and heard his zipper and belt buckle opening. A little voice somewhere in Alex's mind was grateful that he hadn't used his belt on her. She wantonly raised her hips to him, not caring much which hole he took. He chose her cunt, nudging the blunt head of his cock between her lips, spreading her open.

His cock matched the rest of him; large, hard, and more than a match for her. Jordan slid in with a groan. He ground himself in to the root, pushing her further into the bed, then straightened and grabbed her ass with both hands. He knelt upright over her hips so that he could watch his cock thrusting in and out of her.

"Even if you are trash, I can see why Kevin keeps you around... So fucking tight..."

Alex didn't even care about his insults anymore. And it didn't matter if he told Kevin, now he was just as guilty as she was. If Jordan had fucked her, then it would be his cum still inside her ass, the outline of his lips on her clavicle, his cock and hands that had made her pussy wet all along. Terry, Derek, and Tomás would be non-entities.

Jordan's fingers played with the place where their bodies joined. The angle of his thrusts made the head of his cock rub hard against that magic place inside her that was running her every thought at the moment. She felt an orgasm building but resolved to stay silent. She would not give him the satisfaction of knowing when she came.

All the same, there was no way to disguise the way her body rippled as pleasure crashed over her. She knew Jordan could feel her pussy flex and relax around his cock as he pumped inside her.

"Filthy cunt," he growled. His hands kneaded at her ass cheeks. He started to spank her again, in time with the motion of his hips. Alex grabbed handfuls of the sheets and whined into them.

When he came, he pulled out and deliberately ejaculated all over her hot, red ass. He delivered a few final slaps to the backs of her thighs, did up his pants, and walked out, leaving Alex to pick herself up and totter into the nearest bathroom without being seen by someone else. Now she looked a mess. Her makeup was ruined and her curls had turned into a mop of limp waves. She dabbed off her eye makeup and patted her face with tissues. Her hair she put up in a bun. Looking at herself, she could believe that she had been fucked by several men that night. Alex washed her face with cold water and drank a quantity of it as well. She helped herself to some lotion from a cabinet and made her way downstairs. Some people had left, but there were still plenty of partygoers milling about. Alex claimed a bag of pistachios, a can of soda, and slid quietly into a place on one of the couches. Barely anyone noticed her.

Alex had her face pointed in the general direction of the TV screen, but her eyes quickly diverged into the middle distance while she munched and sipped. The evening played like a movie in her head, a drunken reel of disjointed images and sounds. She was exhausted and achy, but she knew this would happen again. How soon, she didn't know. Or with who, or how many. Alex reached for a box of cookies on an end table. It was time to relax, recover, reflect, and eat cookies.

When she and Kevin left the party, he acted like she'd only been gone a moment. She felt a twinge of scorn when she asked her if she'd had a good time, but pasted on a sweet smile and answered truthfully – yes, she'd had a very good time.

He frowned. "Weren't you wearing tights earlier?"

"Um, I snagged them on something and had to take them off." He accepted that.

When they got to Kevin's apartment, Alex didn't think she'd be in the mood yet again, much less for Kevin, but something inside her felt sorry for him. She knew she was exactly what Shane had called her. But Kevin was still happy. Time to think about that later, she decided as she let Kevin position her on her hands and knees and pull her pajama pants down. He pushed two fingers into her. She let out a gasp. It hurt at first, but she was still wet, and pleasure arrived swiftly. Kevin took the sound as pure arousal. That she was already wet for him. He lined his glans up with her opening and pushed himself into her cunt in one stroke. Kevin was never big on foreplay. That used to disappoint her. Now, she was glad.

I am a thing to use and be used, she thought without a pang. Kevin began to thrust. Alex adjusted her stance and arched her back. He liked that. His hands each took a handful of her ass, squeezing them, moving them around. Kevin's thumbs slid near her asshole. He begged her to let him play with her ass. Just a little. Normally, she would tell him no. This time, she asked him to.

Kevin spit on his right thumb and pushed it into her ass. There was a pain there too. But satisfaction that her boyfriend's thumb was now covered in the little bit of Vaseline and semen that were still inside her. He moved it back and forth slowly. When he got closer to orgasm, he held it still while his thrusts became faster and more erratic. When he came, he pulled both his cock and finger out quickly, which made Alex gasp again, and came all over her ass. She stayed in position for a moment, swaying. Now she was truly done.

Alex managed to shower, stumbled to the bed, and fell into it. Kevin was already there.

"Oh!" he said brightly. "Jordan told me he'd hung out with you for a bit." Cold water splashed over her heart.

"Ah, uh-huh?" she answered lamely.

"He said we should have our next get-together at his place."

Alex fought back a laugh. "I think that's a great idea."

Pirithous, Persephone, and the Nymphs

Pirithous's footsteps made little noise on the forest floor. He used familiar routes; old goat trails he could follow with his eyes closed. There didn't seem to be any game to be had yet, so he headed deeper into the woods than he normally did.

The wind rattled in the trees, but when the breeze stilled, there was still a faint noise on the air. It sounded like fluttering. Pirithous realized he was no longer sure where he was. He told himself he could just retrace his steps. These woods were not so large as to get dangerously lost in. The laughter drew him on.

The shrubs parted before him and he came upon a dell, ringed about with old Valonia oak trees, with a small pool at one end, a tiny finger of a spring that branched wide beneath the earth and stone. There was the source of the laughter.

There was a group of girls sitting around the pool, watching two others play in the water. Pirithous ducked back and crouched down. Should he go away and have some respect? Or take a look while he could and then leave? He retreated a few steps and moved sideways to a spot where he'd be better covered. He looked up again.

Those were not girls, he realized – not human girls, anyway. The two in the water were wrestling. They splashed and squealed. Four others lounged around the pool, watching and laughing together. They passed cups of liquor dark and gold around, and a smoking pipe. It smelled like nothing he had ever smelt before. Even from here, it was heady. He looked toward the pool.

There. There it was. That was what was wrong. The girls in the water were half melted into it. Their bodies were joined to the surface. These were not women. Pirithous's heart skipped. He could believe gods and goddesses existed, but nymphs? He'd never made up his mind on those. But he was sure he was seeing them now.

I'm going to be killed, he thought. No one in the stories who sees this kind of thing ever lives. But he could not look away.

They were all different, even the two in the water, at least the parts above the surface. A water nymph is a beautiful thing, but a strange one too. One had hair of gray-blue water that moved continuously in waves from her crown to her breasts, streaked with reeds. Her body was sinuous and not quite opaque. The other was crowned with a sweep of deeper blue with flashes of gold on the surface, and webbed hands. Both had bodies brimming over with curves. Was that a minnow that leaped from an arm?

They grappled with each other, letting themselves splash into the pool and dissolve, then rear up again. They touched in other ways too. One bared sharp little teeth as if to bite her opponent, but sucked on her neck instead. The hand of the other slid over the cleft of her rival's ass. The others shouted in approval.

They bet on their favorite with mushrooms, lumps of amber, coins, and such. Pirithous forced his gaze away from the water nymphs to the others. One was probably a dryad, he reasoned. Tall, straight, and slender she was. Her long hair was a thicket of evergreen needles bound back with withes studded with gray seeds. Heavy-lidded eyelids showed globes of amber inside. Her skin was a light mottled gray. She leaned sideways to speak into the ear of her companion.

The nymph sitting next to the dryad had a rugged beauty, her body all elbows and knees. The blooms that flowed from the crown of her head down to her bottom were an extravagant tumble of light purple. She broke into laughter at what her friend said, and petals rained from her shoulders. Sitting in front of them with her elbows around her knees, was another, smaller flower maid. She was watching the battling water nymphs, unaware of anything else. Pirithous's eyes lingered on her. She was pale pink and soft, with plump thighs. A fluffy pink and white mop obscured part of her face from his angle. Her fingers were dusty green. He turned his eyes to see the last being.

That one. That one was no nymph. Pirithous almost pissed himself. That was a goddess. He had no idea how he knew, but he was surer of that than anything. And he had a good guess which one she was. The Spring Queen. She who swallowed death to feed birth. The Dread One who crossed the veil as she pleased with none to stop her.

Persephone was a wild thing. It was her mother, Demeter, who had the blush of summer beauty. Persephone was the savagery before and beneath. The cries of the foxes, the hunger in their bellies. The winter tried hard to keep its hold, but every year Persephone wrested away control, day by day. Every year, she proved stronger. She was the contractions in the doe that brought the fawn forth, the patience of the green shoots clawing their way through the cold soil to seek the pale sun, light without warmth.

The Goddess of Spring was a small thing, with thin brown limbs. A thick mane of hair fell about her shoulders and back. It was streaked amber, chestnut, and tawny, wound about with budding vines. Her hands and feet were clawed. Around her neck she wore a golden torque set with chips of obsidian and black diamond. Matching anklets dripped gems on her feet. The wife of Hades has the wealth of all that is under the earth at her disposal, and the King of the Underworld worshiped her more fervently than the nymphs she had created did. Other than that, she was as nude as they all were. Soon pollen, the gold most precious to her, would dust her shoulders and flanks.

There was a particularly loud splash. One of the water nymphs had grappled the other onto the bank. The others shouted, clapped, and began to collect their winnings. The petite flower nymph got up off her knees and turned to walk back to her companions. Her heart-shaped ass had a few blades of grass stuck to it. She took two steps and froze. Her ruffled pink head turned halfway to him, and she put her face up to the air. Pirithous's heart sank. She yelped and dashed back to her sisters. She had caught his scent.

Pirithous whirled to run, but the goddess had only to throw up a hand and he fell to the ground. He could turn his eyes enough to see their feet running toward him. They snatched him up and dumped him on the bank of the pool, then retreated a few steps.

He lay still, not knowing what was coming. A single hand took him by the back of the neck, hauled him up, and turned him to face the hand's owner. A few seconds before, he was hiding in the bushes, watching the wondrous scene. Now, he was looking into the face of a goddess, and Persephone did not look pleased.

She was indeed beautiful, but he knew if he looked long at her yellow-green eyes that he would be sent screaming into madness. She took hold of his chin and looked hard at his face. He was petrified. He rolled his eyes all about, but they kept returning to hers. He concentrated on her brow, praying to her in his mind to release him. Her hand was near as small as a child's, but he could feel that it was stronger than iron pincers. Finally, she was satisfied.

"There is no evil in you. No harm in your intentions. But pure? No. Highly impure." She pronounced each word all on its own. Her voice was husky and echoed even in the space between them. "So. You must be cleansed." She turned to the nymphs. "Come, my dears!"

They surged toward him. His arms and legs were seized by hands soft and hard. They pulled off his clothes and dragged him to the pool. He began to shout and struggle. Did they mean to drown him? The two water nymphs rose with their arms open, their smiles wicked. They caught him and the three plunged into the pool. He could no longer tell where the water maids were anymore, but they tumbled him about until he no longer knew which way was up. Finally, they released him. He bobbed to the surface coughing water. The nymphs laughed.

Pirithous struggled up the bank, naked and dripping. Persephone only glided by, the smallest of smiles on her lips. Pirithous shook his head. The beautiful girls were all around him now. Everywhere he looked, there were full breasts, long thighs, and sweet lips. They giggled, and two of them pointed. He looked down. He was sporting an erection.

"My loves," Persephone intoned. "Mortal men may be fools, but you are greater beings, precious to me. Now, introduce yourselves to our catch."

"I'm Cypress," said the dryad. "Also sacred to Artemis."

"I'm Prespa," said the nymph with sun-dappled hair. "Of the lake."

"Halia, of the river," said the nymph with reeds.

"I'm Croce. Your people call me Laconian Thyme," said the purple-flowered nymph.

"And I'm Meria," said the pink nymph, shy again. "I'm rare." The goddess's voice came again.

"Each one of you may please yourself," the goddess pointed at him, "As you will." The nymphs all started talking at once.

"I saw him first!" said Cypress. It was true that trees see and hear much. She and her sister spirits whispered to each other in the wind and joined hands underground.

"If you did, you didn't say so," Meria spoke up. "I caught him because I smelled him and told you all."

"Hey!" objected a water nymph he couldn't see. "We need a little pleasure after all that wrestling."

"Croce, that's not fair!" cried Meria. She pointed down.

"Doesn't matter whether or not the cup is half full," said Croce. While the others argued, she had taken Pirithous by the hair and pushed his head between her thighs. "Unless you drink it."

Pirithous's noises of surprise were muffled but he swiftly got to work.

"Ooh," Croce purred. "He's a good one. You'll like him."

"Ugh. Don't take too long," said Halia.

"Greedy heifer," grumbled Prespa. They settled themselves on the moss to watch. Persephone took out the pipe again. With sleight of hand, she produced a small lump of dry plant matter. A fire sprite appeared to breathe on the bowl and just as quickly vanished.

Pirithous kissed Croce's hood. He slipped his tongue just beneath it and moved it back and forth. "Mmmm..." Her head fell back with a moan. Pirithous licked on while she squirmed on the ground. Cypress knelt next to her and stroked her hair. Halia joined them. She arranged herself on her side and bent her head to lick and suck Croce's nipples. Pirithous slid his tongue inside the flower nymph.

"Ohhh, yessss..." She tasted delicious, like a complex wine. Earth and mint and lemons. Pirithous still had consciousness enough to wonder if there were mint and lemon nymphs. He withdrew from her opening and began to run his tongue in slow circles around her lips, spiraling inward. Her moans grew longer and breathier. Cypress leaned over Croce to kiss her.

"Yes, my sister," the dryad murmured against her lips. "Feel it all." Pirithous applied his tongue in an O around her clitoris and sucked. Halia's hands roamed over the flower nymph's angular frame. Croce's back arched when she came. Soft hands caressed her body, breasts, the insides of her thighs. She sighed into Cypress's kiss. When they parted, she raised herself on her elbows and gave Pirithous a drunken smile.

"All right!" The tree nymph clapped her hands. "My turn."

Before he could get up, Pirithous felt himself seized by many hands? Or fingers? He looked down as best he could. The long gray coils could only belong to Cypress.

"This is for letting her have you first," her voice came. Something whished through the air and cracked him across the ass. Pain lit up his world. Another stroke followed a heartbeat later. "And that's for being a peeper!"

She was lashing him with a switch, he realized. A third blow made him cry out.

"And that's for –"

"That's enough," Persephone's voice came. The switch vanished immediately.

"Yes, my Lady. May I continue otherwise?"

"Do so," the Dread Queen commanded.

Cypress lay back on the ground. The flexible branches turned Pirithous to face her. His cock was still hard. She pulled him toward her. He tried to take her in his arms, but could not. She held him fast, with his cock out in front of him, harder than ever at the sight of her, a beautiful tree nymph with small, pointed breasts and golden eyes. She brought him in.

Pirithous thought he might finish in a few seconds when the head of his cock touched her, but he did not. She slid him into herself with an exhalation like a cool autumn breeze, though it was full spring. She smelled of spice and resin. Cypress began to use him as a toy. She fucked herself with his body. It was a completely alien experience to him. He had been ridden by a woman in pursuit of her own pleasure, but he'd never been restrained, lifted bodily, and become essentially a dildo, a cock with a man attached. It was humiliating. And he never wanted it to end.

Besides, she was doing all the work for him. As he didn't need to support his weight or regulate his thrusts, Pirithous could watch every second. Her cheeks and lips took on a purplish flush from the hot sap under her skin. Cypress's mouth opened and her eyelids fluttered.

She adjusted him so that the head of his cock rubbed against the upper wall of her cunt. Sometimes she moved him slowly, sometimes fast and hard. Pirithous nearly came a dozen times. He didn't know how, but she seemed to know each time, and denied him. Each time she reached orgasm, her legs would spasm and her toes would curl. Prespa reclined next to her, kissing her throat and running her hands over her limbs.

He wanted to touch them so badly. The feeling of Cypress's cunt flexing around his cock was incredible, and he was watching something few, if any, mortal men had ever seen – a tree nymph and a lake nymph kissing, stroking, tonguing each other – yet it was torture.

He could hear the others talking and laughing when their mouths weren't busy otherwise. He smelled the smoke from the pipe. It had notes familiar and unknown. When Cypress was finished with him, she let him go. He stumbled to his knees. His cock was pulsing on the air. A bead of clear liquid formed at the tip and ran down his shaft to glisten on his balls.

"Over here," a voice cooed. Prespa went to all fours in front of and wiggled her ass at him. "You haven't lived 'til you've fucked a water nymph." She spread her knees further and arched her back. Pirithous was done being any more reverent than he needed to be. He grabbed for her.

A water nymph is indeed a wonderful being to fuck. They can accommodate any sized member, yet she still felt as tight as any he'd known when Pirithous pushed himself into her. He didn't waste a second to start fucking her hard. She was so slick inside. He could feel her around every contour of his cock. Prespa's body felt cool within, a new sensation. The slight reduction in sensitivity would only make him cum harder, he knew. Her ass jiggled delightfully as his hips slapped hers.

"More!" she urged. He could see his cock moving in her. Pirithous took her by the waist and slammed them both together. He squeezed her ample buttocks. The golden streaks in her hair danced to the time of Pirithous's thrusts. Prespa looked over her shoulder at him, the deep blue curtain half covering her face, and winked. She reached behind her and slid two fingers into her ass.

"Give it to me," she purred. He withdrew from her pussy and nudged his glans against her asshole. It still took effort to work himself in. The others seemed far away, but he heard one of the nymphs' voices.

"Hahaha, you slut," she giggled.

Prespa only replied with a low moan that went on and on. Pirithous reached down and ran his finger around the spot where their bodies joined. That made the lake maiden gasp. She quickly found her voice and told him, ordered him, begged him to fuck her ass. Pirithous felt like exercising a little cruelty of his own. He pulled back until only the tip of his cock was past the tight grip of her opening, and pushed back in with one long, firm stroke. Not fast, not slow. He did this over and over until he could sense she was getting desperate. He too was nearing the point of no return. He might be punished for it, but so far, if this was punishment, he would dare it.

He pushed his cock into Prespa's body all the way to the root and began making short, fast, deep thrusts. Pirithous raised himself higher on his knees so that he could angle his cock to stroke her womanly passage from within her ass. Prespa's sounds of pleasure grew breathier and higher-pitched. Only a few moments more and a strong climax rippled through her body, making her tighten on him again and again. There was no way he could stand against that. Her body milked the seed out of him in jet after jet. He could just see his spend dispersing inside her.

They detached from each other. Prespa crawled a few steps away and lay on her side, making a hum of pleasure. Pirithous could see a drop of his seed running down her inner cheek. That made a stab of pure arousal go through Pirithous's body, even while he lay there panting with empty balls. But there were still two nymphs left unsatisfied. Meria's voice came.

"You go next, Halia. We all know you're a naughty thing who deserves what she's about to get." Halia grinned at her and strode forward.

"Sit there," she pointed to a rock. Pirithous obeyed. His behind had barely touched the cool stone before the river nymph put herself over his knee. Pirithous sat frozen for a moment, his hands in the air. Halia looked at him sideways.

"Well? What are you waiting for? Spank me!" Pirithous still couldn't quite believe what he was hearing, but he believed his eyes. A lovely water maid lying over his knee, plump ass in the air, looking at him coyly through her curtain of hair.

"Don't think you're in charge, though," she warned. She spread her palms on the ground. Pirithous gave her bottom a light slap.

"Come on, now!" she complained. Pirithous grabbed a handful of her watery hair. If she wanted it rougher, she'd get it. He began to spank her with broad-handed, even strokes. Halia's ass, like Prespa's, had a lovely jiggle to it when struck. She took it with smiles and giggles for a few minutes. Then those became a look of open-mouthed concentration. Pirithous kept smacking her ass and upper thighs. He varied his cadence so that she could never be sure where the next blow would land. A long, low moan was born in her chest and slowly grew until it became a filthy noise. He got an idea.

He put his fingers together and slipped them between Halia's lower lips. Her legs spasmed. It was a good idea. Her back arched. He still had hold of her hair. Pirithous began to slide his hand up and down following the curve of her body. He teased her entrance, grazed her clit, and tickled her asshole. He released her hair. With his free hand, he resumed spanking her round cheeks. The river nymph's toes were waving in the air. Her mouth was open like there wasn't enough air in the whole forest.

The other nymphs hadn't joined in this time. They watched, a couple with grins, a couple with wide eyes. Pirithous slid two fingers into her cunt and his thumb into her ass. When she came, Halia couldn't make a single sound, only spasm over Pirithous's lap. He spanked and fingered her all the way through, until her body went limp. Her sisters collected her and laid her down with her head in Persephone's lap.

Pirithous looked down at himself. He was hard again. He cast his eyes up again. Meria was standing a few steps away, looking at him hungrily, one finger in her mouth. The little pink flower maid sauntered over to a patch of ferns and sat down in the springy leaves. She put her knees up and crossed one leg over another.

"Come here." She crooked her finger at him. He obeyed. Meria extended her leg and pointed her toes. "Worship them." He did.

Pirithous swirled his tongue over her arch and sucked her toes. He massaged her feet with his hands. When she'd had enough of that, she placed the ball of one foot against his chest and gently pushed. She stood as he went down, more graceful than any human could hope to be. She stood over him. Her hand descended to touch herself, her fingers spreading in a Y shape, pushing her lips together, caressing her clit with her own flesh. Meria went to her knees and lowered herself onto Pirithous's face. He grabbed her round thighs and began to devour her. She tasted of melons and rain. It was bliss. His mouth watered at her taste and smell. It joined with her arousal to run down the sides of his face. He drank her up. Pirithous used his hands to grind her against his jaws. When she moved back for a second, he caught a glimpse of her hands handling her full breasts and nipples.

Meria rode his face for what might have been ages or a minute. She loosed herself from his hands and turned around to ride his face in reverse. Her petite frame made it a reach, but she managed. Pirithous grabbed her ass and ate her up. From this angle it was easy to lick her ass as well as her pussy. He almost came again when the flower nymph's delicate lips closed around the head of his cock. His hips began to move up and down of their own accord. Meria swallowed him down to the root. Her little tongue worked at him. He wasn't going to last long at this rate.

She pulled her mouth off of his cock to cry out in climax. Pirithous flicked her asshole with his tongue, making her voice jump. She slid off of him. His cock was still hard. He wanted to cum again. Persephone must have known what he was thinking.

"Everyone," she pronounced. The nymphs turned as one to look at their goddess. "On him. The human has done well. Bring him release again."

Pirithous would only half-remember what happened next. He remembered Cypress suspending him again, this time as if he were lounging on a throne. He remembered Halia's smooth fingers sliding into his ass, Prespa's plush lips around his shaft, Meria's sweet mouth on his, Croce sucking his nipples.

Persephone appeared in front of him. He concentrated on her mouth. It was sweet when closed but contained far too many sharp little teeth. She stepped closer. The goddess smelled of something like melting snow, blood, and distant fires. Pirithous hung there and whimpered. The lips, fingers, and breasts of the nymphs were everywhere, and in front of him the exquisite horror that was the Dread Queen. He wanted to cum so badly. He begged her with his inner voice.

She shook her head. A bumblebee trundled down her arm. Halia's fingers found his prostate. Colors burst behind his eyes. He begged the goddess again. She shook her head. Cypress's mouth left a trail of soft, dry kisses from his ear to his shoulder. Pirithous tried to beg for mercy, but Meria's tongue was in his mouth. Halia twisted her fingers. Meria released him to allow his cry of agony to burst into the air. He begged the goddess shamelessly, promising her everything if she would only grant him release. Prespa's mouth worked at him steadily, pulling his seed up into the shaft of his cock, but it could not release. His balls moved visibly, trying to pump his climax up and out, but it could not.

Finally, Persephone granted him mercy. She reached forward and gave his aching balls a single caress with her hand. Pirithous's mind shattered. Prespa released him to let his ejaculate spatter them in ropes. The nymphs closed their eyes and stuck out their tongues. They licked his spend from their fingers and each other's breasts, necks, and faces. The world faded out.

Pirithous was dimly aware of water flowing over his body, then a wash of warmth that dried him in seconds. Soft hands dressed him. A cup of something warm and spicy was held to his mouth, and he drank deep.

When he woke, he was lying on a bed of dry pine needles. He blinked and looked around. He knew this spot. It was near the place where he usually entered the woods in search of game. A voice echoed in his mind.

You haven't been punished enough. You will see us again.

Saddle-Sore

It was a warm spring day as they approached the Duke's manor. Lisbeth had left off her riding habit. Baron Zoller, a longtime friend of her father, had made sure the last day of riding would be short as they wanted to get there looking fresh, not sweaty and smelling of the horses.

Lisbeth had taken great care in picking out the dress she wanted to be seen approaching the manor in. It was the soft yet rich pink of hydrangeas. She had endless layers of skirts, but each only a flimsy petal. The dress fell gracefully from her shoulders, the bustline edged with pale silver and ecru lace. The sleeves were slim to her elbows, then opened to a froth of the same lace that left her wrists and hands on display. She'd kept them carefully gloved on the journey so they would look soft and fine. The lace was a gift from the Duke. He'd had an entire bolt sent over, and Lisbeth made sure that there was plenty of it around the decolletage of her gown. Her chestnut curls were gently twisted away from her brow, held with a bit of silver ribbon, and allowed to fall over her bare shoulders.

For a while she had disliked the dusting of freckles across her nose and forearms, but had decided to believe what her father told her – that it made her look as healthy and energetic as she was. The Duke would like that, he told her. A lively young thing, not some dour, tired rag. Lisbeth looked down at herself. No one would ever think that of her, with her pert breasts like two ripe apples, slender legs, and round little bottom. It would be a shame that her days of running and shouting and climbing trees were over, but she'd already left that behind some time ago, she told herself. Being a lady was truly much better. It kept her dresses clean and her hair untangled. Now, eyes lingered on her with want, not disapproval.

She was resplendent, almost smug. Her mates were jealous. She knew it and so did they.

There was also a sadness among them. They would not be seeing each other as often. And yet when they did, they whispered, how grand it would be. Because in only a few years, they would all be married ladies with their own fine houses, manors, maybe even a castle or two among them.

Allegra, with her silky golden hair and love of dancing, had the favor of three knights, two of which rode with them now, Sir Lonnis and Sir Hill. All handsome, landed, and courtly. The third, Sir Brennan, had fractured his leg when a tree limb fell on him during a hunt. How Allegra had fussed over him, bringing him cakes and books and kittens, to the degree that the other two knights said extra prayers for their brother-in-arms to get well faster. Allegra would need to marry someone young and vigorous, for none else could keep up with her. As free and fierce as a falcon she was, seeming to skip on the air whether on the dance floor or in the woods chasing rabbits. She would not say boo about it to even her close friends, but there were whispers that she had kissed more than one of the knights at a time, and more than kissing besides. Even so, she'd never been caught at anything, and went about her business with her braid swinging and her lips flushed from being recently kissed by who knows whom.

Cerise, with her sparkling black eyes and bountiful decolletage, had a voice sweet enough to distract attention from her bosom. She was betrothed to a widowed Count. A stern older man, he melted in her presence. He always kissed her hands and pressed some little gift into them – maybe a pomander for her wardrobe or a monogrammed handkerchief with their initials already entwined. Everyone knew that as soon as Cerise's mother was satisfied with her dowry, the next gift from the Count would be a ring. It had been the subject of much whispering among the girls. What would the ring be like? Would it be sleek and classic, like the Count's austere tastes? Or would it be as lush as Cerise, with more than one kind of stone? A ruby, perhaps, or a sensuous pearl, or frosty all over with diamonds? Cerise's older sister had wed an admiral, and he had given her not only a ring, but a demi-parure of rare green amber lifted from the bottom of a shallow sea that hid an ancient, petrified forest, long swallowed by the tide. Now Cerise's Count had a siren nearly within his hands.

Quenthel, tall and willowy with glowing copper skin, was being courted by a rich merchant, a shrewd man who understood what investments were most likely to remain lucrative in times of feasting or fasting. His main choice was wine. They had passed some giggling nights in each other's canopied beds, sipping from flasks of clear, snappy golden cordial or rich black brandy that was almost syrup. It was over these libations that Quenthel had whispered that she wasn't marrying the merchant for all his wine and coinage, or for the fact that he was a jolly, dumpy fellow perfect for a young wife who wanted indulging, no, she was marrying him because of his sister. She and the merchant were a pair. A spinster, she had shown no interest in finding a husband, but preferred to co-rule their little empire. Quenthel's friends knew that she liked girls better than boys, and they had practiced kissing with her. Now their friend would have a husband and a wife. How Quenthel's face had shone when she described the woman's clever hands, how the strong fingers had interlaced with hers. With them she would travel the world.

Lisbeth tossed her curls. It was a pity the girls were not with her right now. It would be much more fun, but this was a noble wedding. They'd been obliged all to go to their homes and prepare their gowns and gifts and retinues. Lisbeth wedding the Duke was far from the only reason they would attend. What better opportunity, other than their own weddings, to be seen looking their best in the fullest flush of youth? It didn't matter that all had their mates picked out. This was about being seen by other ladies.

The last time she, Quenthel, Allegra, and Cerise had been together, they had compared swatches of fabric and sketches of the gowns they'd ordered for Lisbeth's wedding. Allegra's was bluer than the sky would be that afternoon and trimmed with velvet bows. She was having the skirts cut two inches shorter than usual and had picked out a sturdy pair of shoes with a strap across the instep. And matching velvet bows, of course. Allegra wasn't about to have anyone stepping on her hem or losing a shoe on the dance floor. Not on your life.

Quenthel would be gowned in silk the color of a ripe peach, with fine golden chains in her hair and over her arms. Golden clasps on her shoulders secured a fall of sheer silk, a sunset flowing down her back to the floor. The dress was to be cut on the bias and would lie on her like a lover's hands. There would certainly be some people stumbling over themselves in her presence. She planned to wear white gardenias in her hair, adding scent to her impression. Quenthel's hair would have only a small braid over her crown to hold the flowers. The rest would fall in a straight blue-black river down to the small of her back. Lisbeth thought she had never seen anyone with a more elegant gait than Quenthel. Not even the Queen, though she'd never let anyone hear that. Crowds parted before her like water under a ship's bow and closed behind her just as smoothly. Lisbeth was fairly sure that Quenthel could walk across a battlefield and not spill a drop of her rosé.

Cerise would be irresistible in champagne lace with amber silk underneath, and pearls dripping into her cleavage. They were family heirlooms. Lisbeth had seen them in a portrait of Cerise's grandmother. Pearls studded the pins that would hold the beautiful girl's hair. But there was one problem.

"Cerise, darling," Lisbeth said, looking at the drawing, "How is your gown to stay up?"

Her friend only shrugged, smiling sweetly. "I don't know."

"Ask Sir Brennan," Quenthel said. "His leg should be all better by then, but unfortunately for you," she looked at Allegra, "He probably won't dance much." Allegra made a wry face and nodded. "I don't think he would mind at all if you asked him to stand close by you and hold your bodice up," Quenthel suggested.

Allegra's face brightened, and she nodded again. "Yes! Oh do it, do it, please. Only hold your wine glass up and give him a drink from time to time, and he'll be ever so happy. And so would I be to see it!"

"You're not jealous?" Cerise asked, her black eyes wide.

"Jealous of him," Quenthel interjected, her eyes locked on Cerise's nipples, showing through her thin nightgown.

Lisbeth held up a finger. "It's the Count who will be jealous." Cerise giggled.

The next morning, many more giggles and kisses were exchanged, and then all set off to make ready.

She knew it had only been a few days, but Lisbeth preferred to think it had been a long, hard ride over mountains and through deserts. That morning, she had awakened in a large, fine inn, in a featherbed that she shared only with her handmaid, a quiet girl named Meg. She'd eaten a decent breakfast that didn't include anything dried or salted in a barrel. There was even a copper bathtub for her to wash in. Meg scented her bath with rose water and anointed her skin with a touch of sweet almond oil. Lisbeth had even enjoyed the oohs and aahs of the other guests as she descended the stairs from her room in her gown, looking like a perfect rose.

But there was one problem. Her escort, Baron Zoller. She'd known him somewhat growing up, as he frequently had business with her father, but she hadn't sought his company. Why would she concern herself with her father's cronies? He was a stern man, she observed. Not unkind, but he did not smile at her games and saucy tongue. Mother and Father too had gone ahead to the Duke's manor, as they had been on business close by and there was familial scheming to be done. Her father trusted the Baron well to charge him with her safety, and thus it was he who escorted her, the remainder of their household, porters, men-at-arms, and a few various others to the Duke's house.

It had not been easy traveling with him. Lisbeth had some inkling that she had been allowed much freedom as a child, and not often disciplined. Her few punishments had included being forbidden to go riding for a week or confinement to her room for a day. Once, after she had been angry with a maid for her inability to remove a stain, Mother had made her try to wash it out herself. Lisbeth had never even thought of such a thing, and it truly shocked her back to better behavior when she felt the hot water and lye soap sting her soft hands.

Those were all the punishments she could recall, other than the occasional warning look across the room or table. But this man was a different sort. Just one more day and she wouldn't have to bear his company anymore. He was a surly old man and she could do as she liked. After all, he was only a Baron and she was about to be a Duchess. All the same, it was making her mood foul. They were passing by a grove of trees.

"Ouch!" Lisbeth yelped as a nut fell from a branch onto her head. "Why could we not take a carriage?"

"For the tenth time, Lady," Baron Zoller said, pronouncing each word separately. "Your mother and father had need of at least one for their business, and your great-aunt is frail. Also, it was the best place for your delicate goods." Lisbeth was not satisfied.

"We could have hired one," she said petulantly. She got no reply. That only irritated her more.

"Will you have a new dress made if a bird shits on me?" She regretted the words as they left her mouth.

"I've had it with your nonsense, girl!" The Baron grabbed his riding crop. "Lean forward, over your saddle."

"What do you mean?" Lisbeth put on an indignant tone, but a chill ran through her. He'd finally reached his limit.

"Your father charged me with getting you to the Duke's manor, and you've been nothing but trouble the whole way." He slapped the crop on his gloved hand, leather on leather. "We're not going to lose any more time on your account, so you'll be getting your stripes ahorse." She still could not comprehend. It was too foreign for her to grasp. She heard Meg utter a small "Ohh," sound.

"My s-stripes?" Lisbeth stammered. The Baron stared at her. His neck was bright pink.

"Do you mean to tell me that you've never been spanked?" he asked. She could not answer. He gave a short bark of laughter. "It's true, then! This brat has never had a proper spanking. Captain Harlon, are you hearing this? The Duchess," he snorted, "Has never been so much as slapped on the bum."

"I hear it, Milord," Captain Harlon said with a nod in his direction. If he was a nobleman and not a mere Captain of the Guard, he might have been a candidate for her hand. Approaching middle age, he had the hard body and excellent posture that experience had gained him. His thick fox-brown hair was cut short, as was his beard. His livery jacket was draped over his saddle pommel, and his sleeves were rolled up. There were scars old and not so old on his forearms.

She had heard Lady Bellworthy whispering with Lady Maynard that he was a talented swordsman in another right. Hidden behind a pillar, Lisbeth would never admit why her heart had set to pounding in her breast. She'd never looked at him that way before, but it was impossible not to after that. The smell of leather and oil had never appealed to her before. Now, it was as good as cinnamon. Even though he rode ahead of her, she could see the edge of a smirk on his face. The Baron turned back to her.

"What are you waiting for, wench? I told you to put your belly down and your rump high."

She gasped. Her father had always indulged her, but his friend was a hardened campaigner who had seen battle. She'd never been struck in her life, not once, and never thought she would be.

"You can't! I'm to be Duchess in three days!"

"I can and I will. A Duchess ought to be a gracious lady, not an impudent slattern. Your father is a good man, but he's been too soft with you. Now do as I say."

Lisbeth hesitated. Her horse, a placid gray mare, was tethered to Sir Lawrence's big bay, so there was no way she could escape. She cast her gaze around. There were people all around her! Some hadn't noticed yet, some were suddenly very interested in their fingernails or the trees, but some looked openly. This couldn't be happening...

She forced her body to obey. She was only bending down to pick up a handkerchief, she told herself. The Baron's voice came again.

"Finally. Now hitch up your skirts." Lisbeth froze. A little croak came from her throat. "Do it, or I'll have Sir Hill do it for you." She could see Sir Hill looking at her out of the corner of her eye. He was one of the knights who vied for Allegra's favor. She was sure that the little trollop would hear about it, if not from him then from someone else, and hold it over her forevermore. She wouldn't be the only one. But there was nothing for it.

Taking as long as she could about it, Lisbeth bent forward in the saddle and started to gather her skirts. But when she tried to lift them, her hands seemed stuck fast. The Baron made an exasperated sigh and nodded at Sir Hill. A cry leaped from her throat when Sir Hill leaned over and yanked her skirts up past her waist. Lisbeth sprang up but the knight pushed her back down. Her bodice was scratching against the saddle blanket. That only added a new level of insult.

"Noooooo, don't tear my lace!" she wailed. Baron Zoller only gave a "Ha!"

"Now your petticoats and chemise."

"Baron!" Lisbeth cried.

"Lady Lisbeth!" he called back, mocking. "Petticoats and chemise, up."

Her chin quivered. It was a nightmare. A nightmare. Any moment she would wake up. Sir Hill did not have to help her this time. Her hands shook but she managed to gather up all the layers of fine cloth. Pushed forward, there was so much of it that it was like wearing blinders. She could barely see anything on either side of her.

Lisbeth felt her escort bringing his horse closer to hers. Another undignified squeal burst from her mouth when she felt his large hand reach over and yank down her drawers, baring her ass and thighs to the warm spring air. He tucked the waistband under her legs and patted her bottom with his gloved hand. Her upper set of cheeks were the first to redden when she heard the chuckles and even one surreptitious whistle.

Her attention was quickly diverted from anyone around her when the first blow came down. The riding crop connected with her tender skin with a crack that filled the whole world. Lisbeth screamed out in spite of herself. Nothing had ever hurt so badly. Nothing, surely.

She was wrong. The second strike burned worse, and the third worse than that. The only cover for her shame was the long curls that hung down around her face. With every crack, she heard the crop slice through the air before it made contact. The Baron would give her a few seconds of reprieve, then begin again. The less frequent strokes were harder, and made her cry out. The faster ones were lighter. He seemed to know exactly when the agony was getting to be too much. He was making this last, she realized. She felt her ass jiggle at every impact. It was humiliating. Now she was sure that at least a few of the people around her were enjoying it. Lisbeth craned her neck to look up and to the side. Captain

Harlon was looking at her openly now. He kept his face still but his eyes were focused on every line of bright pink that appeared on her skin.

The motion of the horse wasn't helping either. It made her ass bounce a little even without the crop, and then sometimes she could not help but move a little as her body tried desperately not to flee the pain on her bottom.

This horrible monster who claimed to be her father's friend and trusted counselor made her apologize for every way she had misbehaved during the journey. To Larkin for insulting his cooking, to Mal of Ellebrook for making a face at his pox scars, to Lady Burdock for stealing her scarf. Lisbeth begged forgiveness for cheating at cards – against Sister Cress of Our Lady of the Assumption, no less. Baron Zoller was not a religious man, but he did not approve of taking advantage of nuns. She regretted flirting with Squire Hendricks, especially because the young man was engaged to Steward Orell's daughter, Tala. And last, she was ever so sorry that she said Baron Zoller's horse, a big skewbald stallion named Precious, one-eared and prone to ill-timed bowel movements, was an ugly nag. All the while, the crop rose and fell.

She never thought being spanked would be like this. Lisbeth had heard other girls talking about getting spanked for one indiscretion or another. Once, she had been taking a stroll in the garden with Murielle Desmera, and when Murielle thought she wasn't looking, Lisbeth saw her clutch at her rear. Her face was stiff with pain. Lisbeth had to know. She coaxed the story out of Murielle. Murielle was a smart girl, but a terrible student, and she had shirked her studies one too many times, so her father had beaten her bottom with a belt. Murielle hadn't wanted to show her, but Lisbeth offered bribe after bribe until she reached the right price – a rose gold hairnet. She had to admit that it would look nicer on Murielle's straight, light brown hair anyway. Her payment secured, Murielle had bent over a garden bench and gathered up her skirts. With an abashed sigh, she allowed Lisbeth to lower her drawers and examine the hot pink weals that stood out on her soft flesh. She remembered how her friend squealed when Lisbeth's hand grazed her cheeks. Murielle had not sat down the entire visit. Now she understood.

Lisbeth was sobbing unashamedly by the time he decided she'd been punished enough. She yelped at even the soft linen touching her bottom as her drawers were pulled back up over her red-streaked skin. Eyes squeezed shut, she hung her head and tried to imagine the Duke. Rovar Dennison, Duke of Aledyne. In the portrait, his gray eyes looked kind. They told her that he liked dogs, too, and had a terraced garden with fountains.

"That should be enough," came the horrible man's voice. "Plenty for you to enjoy sitting on during the wedding festivities. Maybe I'll give you a few strokes just before you leave for the church, to keep you sweet. Or maybe I'll send Captain Harlon to do it."

Precious dropped a fresh load of dung. Lisbeth gritted her teeth and planted the picture of her wedding gown in her mind. It was a deep peacock blue silk that would be visible across not only a crowded ballroom, but a crowded village square. There were cloth-of-gold streaks stitched down the skirts and sleeves. When dusk fell and the candles were lit, they would flare like falling stars.

After the wedding service in Saint Helena's Cathedral, she would change into a second gown for the feast and dancing on the noble estates. This one was an emerald green brocade. It would pick up the lights from the sconces and chandelier, and the auburn tints in her curls would bloom against the green. The skirt was full and heavy, made to twirl in so the brocade would ripple. Lisbeth had it made with a simple, classic silhouette that let the fabric and her looks shine. Later, she planned to have her portrait painted wearing it. Surely she would gain a quantity of fine jewelry once she was firmly installed as Duchess, and it wouldn't do to have her gown compete with her jewels – or her figure.

The splendid gown would make her face look even redder if she put it on now.

"And," came the Baron's hateful voice again, "Those little kisses from the crop will show on your flesh for several days. Once the Duke gets you out of those skirts, he'll know exactly what kind of girl you are."

Lisbeth's eyes flew open. He was right. If the Duke wouldn't know, she could have borne it. What would he say when he saw her behind? Maybe she could claim a young lady's nerves about the wedding night, or being overtired from all the celebrations. He would surely respect that. But how long would the marks take to fade away to nothing? If she took care, maybe she could try to lie only on her back or keep her rear covered for a while. Something deep inside her said it was futile. He would see.

What if he did things like this to her? Cold fear splashed the inside of her chest. She wanted to talk back, to scream, to cry again, but she could make no sound for the rest of the ride. Lisbeth occupied herself with rearranging the wispy pink layers of her skirts. One of the ladies rode up on her right and offered her a handkerchief. Lisbeth thanked her sincerely. The manor was coming into view.

Diary of a Girl, B

This is a collection of excerpts from the diary of B, a slave in service to Mistress Cat under Empress Lara. The document is a collected account of B's time in training at The Haus. Some non-essentials have been deleted. Entries are often written over a period of several days and have been arranged for continuity with permission from Mistress Cat.

Today's the day. The day I go to The Haus. Mistress Cat intends to get the most out of her purchase, she said, and she hasn't the time nor inclination to train her own slave yet again. I understand this. I know that I am far from a proper slave yet. I have little experience at much of anything except what I want in my heart. I want to serve Mistress Cat more than anything. I will learn anything I need to learn for her. I will bear anything I must for her.

I cannot describe how it felt to finally be purchased by her. I spent a good while in the Pen, waiting for someone who saw whatever raw potential there is in me. I saw Mistress Cat come and look at us more than once, I think it was at least three times, but she never bought anyone until she chose me. I don't know why she didn't buy me until then but I don't dare ask. It's none of my business. But I can't help wondering.

I am being sent to The Haus to be trained as a proper slave so that I may serve Mistress Cat in the way she deserves, if my human frame and feeble human mind can withstand it. Empress Lara rules The Haus. They say she is the classic iron fist in a velvet glove. I am already terrified of her, yet I sorely hope that I will see her. Maybe she will even speak to me.

I am so excited yet so scared. The Haus is the premiere establishment of its kind in this area. That in itself excites me because it shows how much Mistress Cat believes in me and values me.

I'm to go to bed soon but so much has happened already! Mistress Cat sent a car for me. I was only allowed one bag, and Mistress Cat had had one of her bitch boys pack it for me. I had no idea what was inside. It turned out to contain mostly toiletries and very little else.

I haven't seen any of the grounds except the front lawn and main house, though if I saw nothing else, I'd still be blown away. It had been described to me as a "country mansion" but that's the understatement of the century. It's a splendid old house that could be called a modernized palace. Climbing ivy, turret rooms, antique-style window panes, fine stonework, all of it. I haven't gotten to see much of the main house. No time for that yet.

When I got there, I was directed to a side door in what I believe is called a carriage house. Slaves and other submissives are stationed above and below the domain of the Dommes. A young woman in a classic maid outfit answered, I entered, and that was that. She showed me to a room with several other beds in it. She directed me to the bed at the far end of the room and directed me to bathe and dress in what they gave me to wear. Then, the other slaves were introduced, I was given dinner, and now I'm having some quiet time of my own before bed.

It already feels surreal. I'm sitting here naked on the floor by my bed. We're to sleep naked unless we're menstruating. They gave me two items to wear during the day: a dress and a pair of slippers. The dress is small. The neckline plunges all the way down to my stomach, so it can be easily pulled aside to bare my breasts. There is a waistband, and a skirt that barely covers my butt. The skirt comes up enough for me to be fucked if I bend over and I can tuck the skirt's hem under the waistband. Mine is blossom pink. It looks nice with my long black hair.

This is a Femdom house, of course, but there are a few males around. The female slaves are called Girls, and given an initial, but the men are Worms, and given a number. The four Girls are C, M, T, and H. There are four Worms as well. I share this room with the other Girls. There's one empty bed left. I don't know where they keep the Worms. Maybe underground, where they belong?

The other Girls are coming in. It must be time for bed.

My trials have already begun. It's been an awful and wonderful day. I'll begin with the awful. In the middle of the night, I woke up to light and the sight of all the Girls and Worms around me. The light was only a few candles but it was enough to see everything well. I immediately thought that maybe it was already morning and I'd overslept, or there was an emergency. But then I noticed that they were grinning.

In a couple of seconds, the sheets were pulled off me and I was flipped over onto my stomach. I was just about to start yelling, but one of the girls, I think it was T, grabbed me by the hair and put her face close to mine.

"Don't you fucking scream," she told me. "If the Misses and Mistresses hear, there will be hell to pay. Now be still."

She kept hold on my hair and pulled my head until I looked over the edge of the bed. Before I could struggle, two Girls held my legs down and the other held my arms behind my back. The Worms stood in front of me. They all had erections. T had them draw straws. I almost screamed again when they told me what the long straw meant – and the others.

In short, I was forced to blow three of the Worms to completion. They went by order of seniority, meaning who has been in service longest. Each took hold of my hair like T had and thrust their cocks into my mouth. They forced my head up and down and pumped their hips into my mouth alternately. None of them spoke. Mostly they looked at the floor.

One has a big, thick cock but didn't take long to cum. Two has a fairly large cock too but took a very long time to cum, or at least it seemed like it. Four has a small cock and never got fully hard. His cum dribbled out. Every time they held my head still until I gulped it down. A string of spit hung from my jaw to the floor. It was making quite the puddle, and I'm sure I probably let some of the cum run out of my mouth too.

Three drew the long straw. He too shoved his cock into my mouth. I'd say it was medium-sized, with a prominent head. He's the only one who spoke to me.

"Make it good and wet," he murmured. "Because it's going in your ass next." He facefucked me until he was satisfied, then let go of my head. Everything felt surreal. Was this real? Had I been drugged and was having a particularly vicious dream? Maybe I was just lightheaded from having to take tiny breaths through my nose for several minutes.

I felt one of the Girls, or it could have been one of the Worms, pull my butt cheeks apart and spit on my hole. The Girls let go of my legs while Worm Three climbed onto my thighs. They made sure never to leave a single second when I wasn't restrained. Three knelt over my upper thighs and grabbed my ass. He kneaded my flesh and started pinching me. Four times he pinched me hard on my butt. I realized it was probably because spanking would make noise. Then he started rubbing his glans in circles around my hole. I shut my eyes. He started pushing. I couldn't help but tighten up, which made it hurt all the more when the head of his dick made it past my outer ring. I couldn't keep myself from whimpering, so C moved over and stuffed a cloth into my mouth.

Three spat on my asshole again and pushed his cock the rest of the way in. C put the cloth into my mouth just in time, because then I really did scream. I wasn't ready for this. Mistress Cat would finger my butt sometimes, but I'd never had a man's hard penis in me. She'd never even plugged me. Mistress told me that she wanted to send me to The Haus with my asshole a little pink pucker and have me come back with a more mature, flexible bloom.

If this is how anal is, then I think training might be long and difficult for me. Three fucked my ass for what was probably only five minutes, but it was the longest five minutes of my life, at least up to this point. He started slowly, moving his dick back and forth in me. Not for long, though. He spat on my hole again and started fucking me harder. I whined around the cloth. Three lowered his body until he lay over me on his elbows. The side of his face was against mine.

"No matter what, you're a slave like the rest of us," he whispered in my ear. We Worms made our choice, just like you. Never, ever, ever think you're better than us, or one night, when you're not expecting it, we'll do this again. And it'll be all four of us. However many times we want."

He went quiet again. For a while, the sounds in the room consisted of the girls giggling and whispering to each other, my muffled sobs, and the soft panting of Three as he used my ass. He had only to move his own ass up and down to fuck mine. I tried to take my mind away from the buttfucking I was enduring. I tried to listen to the Girls.

One told the other to finger the Worm in the ass, and I think she did. Three started breathing harder against the back of my neck. His dick moved up and down, and up and down. My asshole was still trying desperately to expel him. I couldn't make it stop, though it only made the stretching hurt worse. It stung, and was worse when he pulled it back than when he pushed it in. The saliva was enough to let his cock move freely but not nearly enough to make it close to comfortable for me.

The other Girls whispered encouragement to him, sometimes ordering him to go faster, slower, shallower, deeper. He straightened up onto his knees and grabbed my hips. He raised my ass into the air and fucked me with strokes that rubbed the back wall of my cunt, mixing a bit of pleasure with the discomfort. It didn't help. It only felt obscene. My struggles were only small jerks. I must have looked pitiful, only able to fight for an inch or two, but my body was still trying to get his cock out of my ass.

Finally, he was done. He pulled out as he went in, in one stroke. I was sobbing by then. I reminded myself that I was doing this for Mistress Cat. That meant I could handle it.

They took their hands off me and I was free. Free to lie spread-eagled on the bed with my head still hanging off the edge. I could feel my asshole opening and closing on the air, with his ejaculate leaking out. I was grateful for my hair hanging down, obscuring my face. I could barely make any sound anymore, even when a Girl called M pulled the cloth out. Someone patted me on the ass, they blew out the candles, and that was it. I heard the Worms shuffle out of the room and the Girls climbing back into their beds. My body raged but my mind felt numb. For some reason, I fell asleep within a few minutes.

This morning, the other Girls and I were taken to a washroom, the one I'm to bathe in each day now. There is a bathtub big enough for several people and shower fixtures in the ceiling. All open, though. No private bathing.

I still felt sort of mentally numb. I could look at the other Girls in the face but not in the eyes. I looked sort of through them. My asshole stung horribly, like I'd had a baseball bat shoved into me. When we were done, I put on the little pink dress and slippers.

We were taken to a big servant's kitchen and given breakfast. I had some yogurt, fruit, an egg, and some coffee. A smartly-dressed woman I hadn't seen before appeared in the doorway and called for me. I wiped my mouth and went to her quickly.

While we walked through a hallway, the woman told me she was taking me to an audience with Empress Lara. I must have gasped, because she looked at me and told me not to be scared, just on my best behavior. She said that I should kneel in front of the Empress as soon as I entered the room and keep my eyes on the floor until she directed me otherwise. I nodded without saying anything. My eyes must have been as big as the sconces that glowed along the walls.

The Empress's study is straight out of a movie. Rich wood, shelves of books all along the walls, a grand clock, a huge desk, and beautiful fabrics in a theme of bottle green. The Empress herself is, in a word, sumptuous. Empress Lara has creamy olive skin and wavy blue-black hair. She's so very, very curvy too. I probably raised my eyes higher than I should, but I stole a look around as the smartly-dressed woman ushered me into the room, before the Empress could turn around. I must have frozen for a second, as my minder poked me in the middle of my back to push me forward. I tiptoed over slowly and knelt in front of Empress Lara's wingback chair. Her throne.

The air was icy on my skin. My pink dress is short enough so that when I kneel, my bare ass rests on my legs. I kind of like it. It reminds me just how exposed I am. I felt the Empress's gaze from somewhere far above me. I concentrated on her shoes. Dove-gray T-strap heels. If I cast my gaze up a little higher, I could see the hem of her skirt. Plum. My handler introduced me. There was half a second of silence, then I felt a hand on top of my head. It did startle me, but I didn't jump. The Empress stroked my hair.

"Hello, Bella. Our little B." Her hand took me by the chin and lifted my face gently. I kept my eyes down, but she told me to look her in the face. I did. The Empress has hazel eyes, a Roman nose, and sensuous lips. I was instantly in love. Mistress Cat is my one and only, but the heart loves what it loves, and perfection is a many-splendored thing. Mistress Cat taught me that. Another time when I am reminded that she is wise. My pussy was getting wet. Empress Lara inspected my face as if she knew exactly what she was looking for. She said "Yes, yes," and nodded. When she was done, she nodded to my minder and directed me to go with her. While her head was turned, I noticed that the plum fabric was part of a delicious 1940's style skirt suit. Her jewelry was a mix of pearl, silver, and rose gold.

The Empress says that my training will be overseen by Haus Mistress Beryl but much of it will also be done by her subordinate, Miss Anita. Miss Anita is the one who walked me over. She seems solemn, and I don't know what to make of that. She's about my height, thin, with light brown hair. I wonder what kind of teacher she'll be when it gets to the more physical stuff. I didn't meet Mistress Beryl today.

When the Empress said we could go, I heard a small sound. I couldn't resist turning my head to look. In the corner of the room nearer the door were two people I hadn't seen. A Girl, the small blonde called H, knelt on the rug, playing with one of those little metal puzzle toys. She had a leash and collar on, connected to the leg of a side table. There was a carafe of what was probably wine on the table, and some stemless goblets. Beside it was a French press and cups. The leash was long enough so that H could rise on her knees, pour a beverage, and take it over to the Empress. Behind H, a Worm knelt in the corner with his face to the wall. His ass was blistered red, and I think I saw a plug too. He was still shaking. Empress Lara or someone else must have beaten him not a few minutes ago.

Miss Anita showed me the areas of the house that I'm allowed to see at this point. I can't describe it all right now, but I know I'll become a lot more familiar with the place. It's all so splendid, even the humble places. I can't imagine all that's happened here. And the places I haven't seen must be something indeed. I wonder how many playrooms there are and what's in them. I have to stop now.

Miss Anita took me back to the servant's kitchen where I had lunch with the rest of the Girls – chicken and vegetable wraps – and then she took me to the back porch and gave me a document. The Rules of The Haus. She told me to take a walk around the grounds and read it. She marked the places that are most important to me for now. I was glad that I was to walk around. I didn't want to spend too much time sitting today. My butt still hurts some but I can tell it'll be better in a day. I wandered between shady trees while I read the Rules. I want to make sure that there are a few pieces I know really well, so I'm going to rewrite some of them here to make sure I get it. I can't put them down in order from my head just yet.

Under the Empress, there are five Mistresses: Mistress Athena, Mistress Kells, Mistress Beryl, Mistress Nadia, and my Mistress Cat. Like my Mistress, they all have their own house. Each is different. My Mistress is currently keeping me as her only slave, but she says that once I am sufficiently trained, she will get another. I dare to think that it would be wonderful to have a sister slave, a Girl, and a Worm for us all to abuse. One or two Mistresses will stay at The Haus for periods to train their submissives, train new ones belonging to others, hold events, etc. Mistress Cat tells me that she has spent periods at The Haus doing different duties. I hope she will tell me more about them.

Every Mistress reports to Empress Lara. They do not authorize all of their decisions through her. The minor day-to-day things are written down and presented to her periodically. Serious decisions like taking a sub on or letting them go, must be authorized personally by the Empress.

Under the Mistresses are women who are Mistresses-in-training. These are called Misses. It is presumptuous of me, but I already know that I would like to be a Miss one day. A Mistress might have multiple Misses under her, one, or none. My Mistress Cat has no Miss at the moment. There are three Misses here: Miss Josephine, Miss Serenity, and my Miss Anita. If allowed by their Mistresses, Misses may go to other houses or The Haus on whatever business. I caught a glimpse of two women that I believe are the other Misses while Miss Anita was walking me along. I only find them more intriguing by the manner of their dress. A Miss is still firmly under the control of her Mistress, yet they are afforded dignity, something we slaves do not have nor deserve. I hope one day that I will have lost my concept of personal dignity. Although, if I am to be a Miss one day, that would be something that I would likely have to relearn. But how wonderful to relearn such a basal concept within the framework given by one's Mistress.

A Mistress decides what her Miss will wear but the Miss is free to put forth things she likes to be approved or rejected. Today, Miss Anita wore this close-fitting dress of navy blue leather, high-necked and long-sleeved, but almost as short as my dress. Real, soft leather, not thin and artificial. Her slender legs are covered with sheer stockings, and her shoes are sharp little high-heeled booties the color of distant sands.

Then there are us Girls. We can be called just "Girl" or an initial when addressed, though of course our Mistresses can call us anything that they please within their houses. We fall under the definition of submissive and the subset of slave. Many would say that because we have no rights, that we are in danger, that we are being abused, that even if we claim to be happy, that we live in misery. Not so. The parameters within which we operate are as strict as the rules therein. We are never forced to bear more than we can, though our limits may be tested at any time. We are well attended to. Though we are often naked, we do not lack for warmth. Though we are often forced to hold a position for a long time, we remain uninjured. We are never denied water or bathroom use. We may use our ultimate safeword at any time. But if our lifestyle changes us to the point where all of that sounds foreign? That is our responsibility.

Girls do not have to kneel to Misses and may make eye contact. We must adopt respectful stances like standing with our hands held palm-up in front of us, or held behind us. We must defer to Misses in speech and action and show them every courtesy. They in turn train us on how to address everyone and how to act around them. Misses, when teaching Girls or when in charge in general, often carry violet wands to give quick shocks to make us focus. Mistresses often carry violet wands too, as well as small paddles, whips, crops, etc.

I'm learning so many things. I haven't gotten to practice hardly anything though. I must be patient. To make sure I have it, I'm going to put down some more items from the Haus's Rules.

Sometimes Girls will be in chastity, but in minimal, comfortable silicon or leather belts. However, it's always a possibility that something less comfortable may be worn as a punishment. How awful unsoftened leather would feel, or metal.

Cunnilingus will be a big part of any Girl's day. Skill and practice are expected.

- We may perform cunnilingus on each other if we are so inclined, have free time, and have not been directed to abstain by a Mistress, directly or through a Miss.

- We will perform cunnilingus on guests at the guests' direction. This can include serving them orally while Haus members entertain them in the parlor, under the table during dinner, tea, parties, meetings, in bed, as a prelude to other pleasures, as an accompaniment to other pleasures, etc.

- We will perform cunnilingus on any Mistress at her direction unless we are under restriction by our own Mistresses. We may say so to the Mistress commanding us, but if she demands we serve her still, we must do so and will be held blameless. However the Mistresses want to hash it out between them is not our business.

Analingus is a part of our duties as well. Girls will perform analingus under the same parameters as we do cunnilingus. We may do so on each other if we wish, if we have free time, and have not been directed to abstain. Girls will perform analingus on guests at the guests' direction unless under restriction. Girls will perform analingus on any Mistress at her command unless we are under restriction by our own Mistresses. We may say so to the Mistress commanding us, but if she demands we serve her still, we must do so and will be held blameless.

I should note that a guest can demand any sexual acts that are within our total limits. If we have been directed not to do so by our Mistress, we must mention this to the guest, but if they insist, we must obey them and will be held blameless by our Mistress. This is both a demonstration of our loyalty, the oversight of the Mistresses, and a way to demand that guests show integrity when being hosted by The Haus. We must perform oral service on visiting male Dominants as well, under the same rules I already put down.

I will undergo extensive anal training at The Haus. I understand now that what was done to me on my first night there was nothing more than hazing. I believe that one day I will be thankful for it.

Soon, I will be trained on how to clean and maintain my ass. I resolve now to learn that well. Soon, I too will be treated like the other Girls when it comes to my ass. From studying the document, these are some of the requirements concerning anal at The Haus:

- We will be taught how to douche and will give ourselves enemas through instruction and demonstration.

- Our diets will encourage healthy digestion and elimination.

- We will be taught to keep ourselves lubricated to better withstand the occasional finger or such intrusion. It is understood that we are to receive additional lubricant if our asses are to be used any further.

- A couple of the Girls are plugged at all times. A Girl is plugged for as much time as her Mistress desires. Some Mistresses don't feel the need to as it is not necessary, but I suspect that others never want anal penetration to get too comfortable for their slaves or simply consider it part of good discipline, a reminder of their position and purpose.

- Girls are subject to having their anuses and rectums inspected at any time. This will usually be done by a Miss as a form of maintenance. The stance we should automatically adopt is standing bent slightly forward but not so much as to compromise our balance, feet apart, pulling our ass cheeks open.

- We can be pegged, fingered, or toyed anally or vaginally at any time by those with authority to do so.

I'll put down more later as I keep learning.

I've been learning about and observing the Worms lately. These are the male slaves. They are on the lowest rung, of course. They are called "you" or a number when addressed. The Worms exist to be used. They have the fewest limits of us all, and this being a Femdom house, that can only be expected. There are many things a Worm is to do and also many things they are not permitted to do because it is above their station and possibly their capabilities. Remembering pieces of the Rules off the top of my head, these are some things Worms are for, what they do and don't do, etc.

- Worms aren't to be any more visible to guests than is necessary.

- Worms are often kept in chastity cages. These are usually metal and may be part of maintenance, a punishment, or as preparation. These can be put on by and/or at the direction of a Miss or by a Mistress through her. Sometimes Girls are allowed to carry out tasks such as these under supervision. I would like to cage a Worm.

- Worms are also to maintain anal hygiene and be ready for inspection or use at any time.

- Worms are often plugged as part of maintenance or other purposes. Large plugs and/or insufficient lubricant are a frequent punishment for Worms. Vibrating plugs are sometimes used as a reward or for the amusement of the one who ordered it.

- Worms may be ordered to perform analingus on each other at any time, and it is one of the few sexual acts they are allowed to do independently with each other.

- Worms are honored to be objects for the Girls' pleasure. They will perform cunnilingus, analingus, and any other acts we wish them to on us.

- Worms only get to sexually service the Misses as a great reward granted by a Mistress.

- Worms are often collared and leashed. When not in use, they're often tied to a piece of furniture.

Today, I found out that everyone has their own collar and leash. I will get mine soon. Miss Anita said that some subs from Mistress Kells's house are being punished right now for not making them quickly enough.

The Haus is female-ruled but there will be the occasional male Dominant coming to visit. They must be treated with the same deference due the Mistresses, but no one is above the Empress here, not even a guest. The Misses will serve them, but only specific tasks as directed by their Mistress. We Girls will serve the guests with the duties we do around the Haus, and perform whatever sexual acts they require, but only within the bounds of what our Mistress says. For instance, first-time guests are rarely allowed to take a Girl anally. But the Worms? They have no decorative aspect and are function only. They do all that is in the background or beneath a Girl's station. They are to attract as little attention as possible. Guests can do as they please with them as long as they are not injured unduly. Guests can punish the Worms too, and subject them to various treatments as amusement. Guests will often bring their own Girls or Worms for whatever reason. Worms brought by a guest are only deferred to by The Haus's Worms, and then not much. It is a boon to the Haus to have not only other Dominants but submissives pass through it so that we can all be educated to our best potential.

Girls often torment the Worms and play little pranks on them. If we are caught by a Miss and they think we are being too harsh with them, they may report us for punishment and our Mistress or the presiding Haus Mistress will mete out any discipline she sees fit. But it seems to be mostly ignored.

I resolve today that I will take revenge on the Worms, especially on Three. I mustn't rush, as it needs to be right and I need to pull it off. But I mustn't procrastinate, either. You never know when someone might be lent out. They could even leave, be sold, given away, die, and all that. I'll get to planning.

There's so much more I'm doing and learning but I'll have to put it down later.

Today, I had a session with Miss Anita where she taught me more about the Empress and the structure of the place.

Empress Lara has her own Girl we haven't met yet, Q, who is on loan to a personal friend. Miss Anita showed me a picture. Q is a classically beautiful Vietnamese woman. In the picture, she was dressed all in black latex so shiny you could start a fire by bouncing the sun off of it. She is a Mistress herself, but is Empress Lara's Girl. I hope I get to meet her, and I hope she might even give me a command one day. Should I even dare to?

I still haven't met Mistress Beryl, but Miss Anita showed me a picture of her. Mistress Beryl is beautiful too. Nearly as black as Empress Lara's hair, with long, soft locks with little gold ornaments here and there. Her style of dress combined androgyny with luxury. In the picture, she wore a sharply-cut blazer in a color that is hard to describe. Like bronze, but with a little red in it, like it was under candlelight or a sunset. The fabric looked like raw silk. A blinding white buttoned shirt and skinny tie in a shade of deep wine. Cheekbones to slice apples with.

Miss Anita said that the Empress may give direction to anyone at any time that supersedes all others. One may say that they are on the orders of the Empress if challenged. But if you lie about that, life will get very hard for you.

That's all she told me about that, but I already knew some of it. At least, unless the slave who told me was lying. I met N at the auction. I had already been chosen by Mistress Cat but not picked up yet. We were whispering to each other while she waited to be called. N said that she knew a Worm who used to serve at The Haus who committed a grave sin. A guest, a visiting male Dominant, had wanted to use the Worm's ass. The Worm had been cleaning the guest's room naked, and the visitor had liked the look of their clean hole and plump ass cheeks, so he took the Worm by the scruff and bent him over a desk, as was his right. The Dominant was taking his cock out when the Worm not only spoke up but begged the guest not to assfuck him. The Dominant was a considerate sort and deigned to ask a Worm why he did not want to be assfucked. N was not sure why the Worm protested. He had told her it was because he had been used already and his hole was sore, but N had her suspicions. She thought it was more likely because he had been lax in his hygiene or something even worse. She hadn't wanted to say it but I pressed her. N told me that it might have been that there was still a place in him that had not yet made peace with being penetrated by men. I was a little confused. Had he never done it before? I asked. N wasn't 100% sure but thought he had. At the end of the day, she wasn't sure, and I suppose the reason doesn't matter. But he didn't just ask the Dom not to fuck him, she continued. The Dom could still have fucked him, and she didn't know if he had gone ahead with penetrating the Worm or not, but what N did know was that the Worm invoked the Empress's name. She had put no such restriction on the right of a guest to use his ass.

At that, my mouth dropped open and my eyes must have been huge. I never thought anyone would do that. I'm not sure how the Empress heard about it. Maybe the Dom had gone to her to ask her to lift the restriction or because he found the Worm rude in the way he gave his request. Maybe the Worm confessed, or told it in confidence to a Girl or another Worm. If that was the case, I would have told on him too. It was a grave insult to both the guest and Empress Lara. It was an insult to The Haus, period. Thankfully, the guest Dom was gracious. He was immediately given their best, or at least not-so-worthless, Worm to attend him, plus two Girls. He would have been reprieved of the presence of any Worms, but he enjoyed penetrating a male anus, and so was given a willing one. N remembered that the Dom had given it to him hard, and often. She remembered hearing the Worm's groans in the hallway outside the room. She confessed that she had called another Girl over to listen and giggle behind their hands. I think I too will enjoy hearing the sound of Worms being used.

But I had to know the important part: What happened to the sacrilegious, lying, filthy Worm? N's face had scrunched up. It was so terrible, she said. There wasn't much time left. I begged her to tell me. She hesitated, then let it all out in a rush. With actual approval from the Empress, the Worm was sent to a brothel run by an associate where he was offered as the main cumdump for a whole week. In my head I saw a Worm strapped prone to an X or maybe a padded sawhorse, unable to move, maybe unable to even make a noise, while a cock abused his ass like he was an unusually large fleshlight. Or even worse, what if they made him act like he liked it? Maybe he learned to like it. If he had any brains, he would, although he lied about the word of the Empress. Not a smart move. Even now, he might have his arms bound behind his back, bouncing on a cock, his whines muffled by a ball gag.

When the week was up, the Worm was given medical care including STD testing and sent back. He wasn't allowed inside The Haus when he came back, but kept in an outbuilding until they could find someone who wanted him. N had no idea where he'd ended up. One day he just wasn't there anymore. Thing is, anyone who buys a slave, Worm, Girl, or any other type is given their history. Anyone who buys that Worm, if anyone did and he wasn't just released onto the street, would know what he did. He might be a cumdump forever. And it didn't have to be a flesh-and-blood penis abusing his rectum. He would probably be toyed frequently as well. If there were Girls around, heaven knows what they would inflict on him. Well-behaved Worms might too.

At the time I'm writing this, C told me that one of the Worms had been recently punished by a Mistress that another Worm particularly loved. Later that night, the offender had been knocked down by the faithful Worm. He'd been plugged that day. The faithful Worm yanked it out and immediately replaced it with his cock. He buggered the offender mercilessly until he ejaculated in his ass, then shoved the plug back in, forced the Worm who had offended his mistress to clean the lubricant and Wormy cum off his cock, and left.

N and I both agreed that he'd deserved whatever he'd gotten. All Worms should get all that they deserve. It's not for us Girls to decide what that is, but it is always our hope that the Misses, Mistresses, and maybe even the Empress will let us witness them carrying out their judgment, maybe even help carry it out.

That's all for right now. I know I've promised a few times to put down more about what I'm doing and what I've seen, and I will, but there's too much now. I need to put down all that I can and save the rest for when life quiets down a little bit and a routine sets in. Miss Anita tells me that every day will still be different, but that things will get more familiar over time. I still don't know how long that will be.

Lately, I've been thinking about the punishments I'm learning about, and a few I've already seen. There seem to be a few constants:

- Even if a slave is well trained anally and has kept up their maintenance, anal discomfort of some kind is often an effective form of punishment.

- There are some punishments that could be administered to a Girl's cunt, but at The Haus, womanhood is sacred. The outside may be punished in some ways, but the inside is a place of joy. To be denied womanly pleasures like cunnilingus, performing and/or receiving, is a much more common punishment for a Girl.

- Figging is not an uncommon punishment, but it is a nasty one, and leaves little behind. The punisher takes a lump of raw ginger that a Worm or a Girl has peeled and inserts it into the punished one's ass. The ginger is often frozen so that the cold will be another element of discomfort. The melting ginger also produces water that will further irritate the anal tract.

- Lubricant control is simple but effective as well. Even just a few brisk jabs with a dry finger can be the reminder a slave needs to shape up, although I have seen that done on a whim as well. Recently, I saw Miss Serenity stop a Worm in the hallway and bid him to stand still. She had him put his hands on a sideboard. She reached into her pocket and pulled out a glove. I admit that I should not have been watching, but I could not look away. I secreted myself behind a partition and watched as she put the glove on and inserted two fingers into the Worm's ass in one push. He did not scream, but did rise onto his toes, shaking hard. I was close enough to see his butt cheeks clench. Miss Serenity put her hand on his shoulder and pushed him back down. She twisted her fingers inside his ass. She punished him for his indiscretion, she said, by giving him three extra thrusts. When she was finished, she pulled her fingers out sharply, and tossed the glove at him. She then turned on her heel, and walked away. The Worm stood there with his head down, holding his ass like a spanked child.

- Painful substances may be used as lubricant. The Girl called M got punished like that recently. I'll put more about that down later.

- Getting fucked in the ass by a Worm is a terrible punishment for a Girl. I haven't forgotten the punishment I owe the Worms.

- Licking cum out of a Worm's ass is a neutral act for a Worm but a terrible punishment for a Girl. I shudder when I think about that. I hope I never, ever have to do that. It's usually a Worm that will eat any cum that leaks out of a Girl, unless the Dominant present of whatever type does not want a Worm in their presence and chooses to use a Girl.

I have seen some punishments carried out recently. Yesterday, we were eating lunch, and Miss Josephine came in and told us to finish our food quickly and come to the billiard room. I had never been to the billiard room before and immediately felt excited. I drank the last of my soup, grabbed a buttered roll, and left with the other Girls.

The billiard room is, again, like one in a movie. Picture a billiard room in a grand old Victorian-ish house, and that's it. On the playing table were two Worms. They were on their backs, trussed up like turkeys, with their feet up and their asses on the edge of the table. One of them had a hot pink-streaked bottom, the other had no discernable marks.

Miss Josephine stood to the side, tapping a cane on her open palm. We lined up against the wall at a gesture from her.

Miss Josephine has close-cropped green hair and two prosthetic legs of the thin metal kind, the ones that gently curve backward and have ends that look like they should be too small to walk on. She explained to us why we were there and what was going to happen.

A Worm had gotten caned for being clumsy. This particular Worm was aroused by being caned, so he had gotten an erection that persisted throughout the punishment. Miss Josephine left him alone after that, and he had stayed bent over the table, red-assed, naked, and weeping. Another Worm had come in and soothed his fellow by licking his asshole. But the beaten one was still aroused, and climaxed from the other Worm's attentions. The Miss had come back. The Worms had been wrong (no surprise) and she hadn't been finished with the clumsy one. She saw the first Worm's rapidly wilting cock and his companion kneeling behind him and knew immediately. It was not disallowed for them to perform analingus on each other. But it is forbidden to climax without a Mistress's permission unless orgasm is granted at certain intervals or at the completion of certain tasks. The Worms are all equally worthless, but some have earned certain rewards or privileges.

I stood there, listening. I was feeling very self-conscious in this room with my roll in my hand. I tried to shuffle behind another girl and eat it quickly while not standing out.

Now that we knew what was going on, Miss Josephine said that we were to stand and observe quietly while they were punished. I couldn't quite see their faces, but I judged them to be Worms One and Four. Miss Josephine told us that since Four had already had his ass caned, that he would receive a different punishment. His would start first. Afterwards, she might punish them both another way if she felt like it. Miss Josephine directed T to a mini-fridge. T retrieved a lump of frozen ginger about the size of an egg and a small tub of petroleum jelly. Miss Josephine said that it would be a good exercise for us to have T administer the punishment. Under her direction, T coated the ginger with petroleum jelly and placed it against Four's anus. She looked to Miss Josephine, and the Miss nodded. T started pushing. She twisted the ginger back and forth as she pushed.

I saw Four's toes curl up tight and their fingers turn into hooks. A smile formed on the edges of T's lips. She took better hold of the ginger and pushed harder. It popped inside and the Worm howled. Miss Josephine tapped him on the balls with the cane and told him to be quiet. She motioned T back. I swallowed the last of my roll.

Miss Josephine began to use the cane on One's ass. He tried his best to stay still, but before long he was making little movements back and forth. How pitiful they looked. Curled up like shrimps. I could now see the looks of agony on their faces. Their punishment had just started. If it was that bad already... I grimaced. Stroke after stroke, Miss Josephine raised angry red lines over One's buttocks. He was fully exposed. His hands were able to grip the edges of the table, and he was holding it tight. Miss Josephine was lashing the backs of his upper thighs too, and it is a testament to her skill that she did not graze his balls. One started to mewl. All the time, I'm reminded why these creatures are called Worms. I am so glad I belong to a femdom house. I felt a twinge. I don't like men. I thought of the Worm N told me about who might not have liked men either, and tried to avoid having his ass filled by a man's cock, only to endure one after the other. I know that Girls are sometimes loaned to other houses that have male Doms and switches, and I've already talked about how guests are served. It is very, very likely that I will serve a man soon. At least they will not include Worms unless I make a grievous mistake. I have already had my ass filled with a Worm's member. Who knows how a real man would use me?

I caught my mind wandering. I really do have a lot to learn. It won't do to let myself get distracted while I'm watching something important.

Miss Josephine seemed to care less about the noise One was making as time passed. She probably wanted us to enjoy it, and from the look on her face, she was enjoying it too. Even though One was receiving the cane, Four wasn't having an easy time either. The figging was doing exactly as it was supposed to. I could see a drop of water leaking from One's asshole. The ginger was melting. I had never been figged before. Even now, it is becoming clearer to me by the day how kind and lenient Mistress Cat was with me before sending me to The Haus. I wonder if she'll be any different when I return. Part of me hopes she will be stricter, although my Mistress will continue to be perfect no matter what.

Four's rectum had to be in fiery pain. I could see his outer ring making little spasms. It reminded me of those involuntary movements I made when Three's cock was in my ass. Trying to get it out. Trying to open one's ass enough to make it stop touching the horrible thing, the freezing coal burning from the inside out. Now he too was mewling.

Not long ago I mentioned a punishment M had gotten when I wrote about figging. I don't know what she'd done to deserve it, but a Mistress had made M coat her finger with muscle balm and finger her own ass with it. Muscle balm can be hard to scrub out from your cuticles and under your nails, so the Mistress wasn't about to do it with her own fingers. M did as she was bid, but the Mistress wasn't done yet. She made M cover a plug in the muscle balm and put it in her ass. She wore it like that for the rest of the day and was allowed a soothing enema in the evening. Even so, she slept on her stomach that night and avoided sitting as much as she could the next day.

When Miss Josephine was done caning One's ass and thighs, she tapped across the room and selected a different cane, this one thicker and not as flexible. She let a few moments pass while the Worms twitched and moaned. She held the cane down at her side as she rounded the billiard table so the Worms could not see it at all. Neither of them expected the whish-CRACK of the cane across the bottoms of their feet. They were positioned close enough together and the cane was long enough to strike all four feet at once. That's another thing I've never experienced. Bastinado. Being beaten on the soles of your feet. I knew that this would not make them have to walk and stand any less, either.

I looked at the other Girls out of the corner of my eye. M and H were wincing ever so slightly. I would bet that they've had that done to them. C and T are watching with looks of pleasure, T more so than C. Miss Josephine didn't seem to care what noise the Worms were making at all. They were both howling as the cane hit the soles of their feet, over and over. Finally, Miss Josephine judged that they'd had enough. She went over to a desk and picked up a phone, an old-fashioned rotary phone. She dialed a number and whoever answered must have been a Mistress. Miss Josephine reported on what had just happened, gave her respect, and hung up. We were free to go. The Girls and I filed out of the room and we went about our business for the day.

Later on, we were ordered to return to the billiard room. The Worms were gone. This time we were received by Miss Anita. She was wearing a shirt buttoned all the way up and tucked into very short shorts. She wore sheer stockings and high boots. When she led us in, I think I saw fresh bruises on her bottom. Instead of parallel lines, the bruises were round and grouped together. A paddle, maybe, or a tawse. For some reason, that really turned me on. Maybe she'd been ordered to let them show, or maybe she was proud of her marks. Or both.

When we entered, Miss Anita had us line up. She called me forward. Cold fear doused the inside of my chest. She told us that Miss Josephine had told her that I had entered the room with food that I dared to eat while we were being shown a lesson and that I had left crumbs on the carpet. I squinted at the spot where I had stood earlier. She was right – there they were, little white spots on the carpet! I had suspected I fucked up at the time but didn't think that anyone had seen. What had given me such a foolish idea? I immediately felt ashamed of myself.

Miss Anita told the Girls that we were about to watch me get punished. It was warm in the room but I was frigid. She ordered me to go to the spot where the crumbs were and get down on all fours. I had to force my limbs to move, but I was able to do it. I heard the sound of wood against ceramic. The canes were kept in a large glazed pottery vessel in a corner of the room. Miss Anita instructed me that I was to pick up each and every crumb, counting them while I did so. For each crumb I would receive a stroke of the cane. I looked down at the crumbs, let out a breath, and started to pick them up. Pain blazed over both cheeks of my ass.

"B!" Miss Anita said sharply. She hadn't told me to start yet. I waited, stock still, until she told me I could move. I picked up the first crumb and said "One." The sting was incredible. I immediately understood why the Worms had trembled and mewled. I wanted so badly to do the same, but I was determined to act in a way that would make Mistress Cat proud, even if she never heard of this. I counted two, then three, and kept going while the cane lit up my entire world with each stroke across my backside. There must have been at least a dozen crumbs I picked up, the last few so small I doubted they'd were visible, but I could not leave any behind. I could not let Miss Anita see that I had done a bad job with this. I had to be properly and thoroughly contrite.

When I alerted Miss Anita that I believed I was finished, she had another Girl, H, come over to inspect the carpet. I held my breath. She could easily say I had not gotten every crumb, and I doubt Miss Anita would have come over and verified her word. H looked over the carpet carefully. I did not meet her eyes, only stared at the floor myself, but I think she was looking at me too.

H told Miss Anita that the carpet was clean. Miss Anita allowed me to rise and let the crumbs fall from my hand into a wastebasket. I gasped when I stood and my flesh took on a new shape. I will admit that I enjoyed looking at my ass in the bathroom mirror as soon as I could get to it. The red lines were exactly parallel from each other. She had spared my thighs and only caned my buttocks. I'm thankful for that.

That was my first punishment.

Now I can talk about the training I've been doing and the actual things that have been going on.

Some of the first training I received is on cunnilingus, which is no surprise. It happens a lot around here. At first I practiced eating the pussies of the other girls as practice, as I am the newest. Most of the time us Girls eat each other's pussies to amuse ourselves and not as formal practice. The other Girls were instructed to criticize me harshly, and they did.

I learned how to curl my tongue to the underside of a Girl's hood and apply pressure. Sometimes I could take a Girl's outer lips between mine. I learned how to pay court to her outer lips and slowly spiral inward more and more until I could slide my tongue inside her. My jaw muscles are still gaining strength. They were frequently exhausted during my first few weeks at The Haus. Sometimes I had to eat my food slowly. I had to keep my jaws well open while fucking a Girl with my tongue. I had to stick my tongue out as far as I could and run it along the upper wall of her cunt, against or as close as I could get. At the same time, I must keep my teeth from scraping her tender flesh at any time by covering the edges of my teeth with the lips of my mouth. These too I am stretching. Sometimes I uncover my teeth and use the fronts against the Girl's pubic bone or directly on her clitoris to create a sort of firm rippling sensation.

More than anything I have studied and am still studying how to pay close attention to the cues of the Girl whose pussy I am servicing. I must recognize her degree of pleasure, which places and movements draw the best response, and what I can do to enhance the experience further and bring her to the greatest climax possible.

I'm now doing well enough with cunnilingus that I am allowed to eat the pussies of Girls who are being rewarded. I hope that soon I might be able to eat a Miss's pussy. I am not yet worthy of eating a Haus Mistress's pussy, though Mistress Cat has allowed me to service her pussy many times. I hope that I will have much improved when I see her next.

Until later.

I need to write more about anal. Like I've said before, it's very important for a slave to maintain their asshole, inside and out. There are two main aspects of anal maintenance for us: cleanliness and training. Anal is something that we practice every day. To get lazy about that is, beyond the disrespect to one's betters, bad practice for oneself. How easily we punish ourselves with sloth.

I have been given instruction on how to keep my asshole clean, and proper equipment is kept in each bathroom. I have learned how to give myself a quick douche and a deeper enema. The day I had my first, we Girls were lined up on our hands and knees one day and all given enemas. If it was one of us learning something for the first time or practicing something we needed improvement on, it was a frequent thing for us all to go through it at once. We looked very nice, I dare to say. A large, ornate mirror was set up for us to watch. We arched our backs and stuck our bottoms up in the air, hip to hip, soles exposed. A Miss supervised, violet wand in hand. A couple of the Worms wheeled in saline stands. Methodically, they lubed our butt holes, lubed the tips of the syringes, and inserted them. I wiggled my ass a little, trying not to stand out. I watched myself in the mirror and liked how the tube swayed in the air. I dare to say that I look good when I'm in my place, being a good little slut, a proper little slave plugged in. After getting us hooked up, the Worms turned the nozzles on.

It was an odd but not unpleasant sensation, having the warm saline flow into my insides. I watched myself and the other Girls while our bowels were filled. One by one, we were let into the stalls to relieve ourselves. I had to wait the longest. There was some embarrassment, but it felt good afterwards. Completely clean.

After that, we were put in front of the mirror again and made to finish preparing our assholes. Miss Anita directed us to finger ourselves slowly until we could get two fingers in without pain. The Worms attended us the whole time with towels, hand wipes, lube, and such. The other Girls are already very good at this, and I study them carefully whenever I see them work their assholes. It turns me on. Their slender fingers moving inside the flexible little rings. It takes me longer than they to get my hole to relax, but that means I get to watch them longer. We do this every morning and before we put plugs in.

I'm still getting used to my plug – I have my own now. The first plug I wore was a basic one that belongs to The Haus. Plain steel. It was cold whenever I put it in, but the tip was small and it wasn't thick, so even at first it was not so difficult to put in. For me, it's not so much pain as a discomfort that rubs against the surface of the brain and demands to be gotten rid of. But it feels so good. Anal has become a thing of sweet, perverse frustration. I realized that when I used my small plug. It gave me a quick burst of confidence that this could be better than I anticipated. When I inserted the steel plug for the first time, I did so lying on my side in the presence of the other Girls under the eye of Miss Serenity. Miss Serenity dresses in pink lace and cold fury. I love her as well. She is already as magnificent to me as the Mistresses, except for my Mistress Cat, of course. I had already watched the other Girls insert plugs into themselves and each other, and it was time for me to show that I could do it myself.

We were in one of the playrooms. This one was a small medical office. I was perched on an exam table. For fun, Miss Serenity had put me in a hospital gown as well. The other Girls were all naked. The Misses are permitted to have their own fun with our training, and Miss Serenity has a flair for the dramatic. I lay on my side with my hips on the edge of the table. A tray lay next to me on the table with the plug, lube, and gloves. Slowly, I went through the steps like I had been taught, working my asshole open with the lube, the glove, and the hand movements shown to me by the Misses and the other Girls. I took my time. I kept an eye on Miss Serenity, but she displayed no signs of impatience. I lubricated the plug and took care to situate the tip against my asshole just so. Having the plug inserted a few times by the other Girls had already told me that the angle of penetration mattered a lot, as did making sure that the very tip of the plug entered straight on.

I tightened my fingers around the base of the plug and began. For a few seconds I would push it inward, then stop, rotate it a bit, push, wiggle, push, pull it out, then start again, getting it in further and further each time, until it slid all the way in. I made it with an exhale that felt like pure peace. I put my head down on the table and breathed. The light was bright on the inside of my eyelids. Miss Serenity praised me and patted me on the ass. She permitted me to rise, wash my hands, and put on my dress, this time a green one.

My plug is beautiful. It's a plump little teardrop that stretches me well each time, but because it's glass, the addition of a little lubricant removes all friction. The stem is thick, so my asshole is always held open. The base is a rose. The color is pale gold, with gold flakes all throughout. Like champagne frozen in glass, carved into a rose, and pushed up my behind.

I have to wear it almost all the time now. One downside to wearing a plug all the time that I would have never considered is the violet wands the Misses carry. They give the insides of one's ass a nasty shock when tapped on the outside of a butt plug. I'm starting to like it.

I got my revenge on Three today. Well, some revenge. I will plan to take more, but I got a lovely cold plate of vengeance today and I'm still enjoying it.

I had a housekeeping job for a few years before finding my calling, and I've used those skills to serve Mistress Cat. It's common at The Haus for a slave to have a particular chore they are responsible for. I was a good laundress, so I was given the chore of washing the Miss's and Mistress's delicates. I don't know who does the Empress's laundry. I know that The Haus does employ a professional cleaning service. The Haus is far too large and we use far too much space and equipment to clean and maintain it all ourselves. It's most likely Empress Lara's Girl, Mistress Q.

I was in the laundry room not long ago. I was naked except for my slippers, plugged, and wearing a pair of nipple clamps. It is not their primary purpose, but I find that the clamps improve my posture, as I keep my arms lower and a little further out in front of me so that they will not make contact with the fragile fabrics. It would not do for my nipple clamps to snag on some lace, and I don't like bumping them too much anyway. I was standing at the slab, shivering a little from the moisture on my body, dabbing away at a stray drop of menstrual blood staining a pair of panties. I heard voices. I could not quite understand what they were saying, but something inside me told me that I needed to hear it. I crept to the doorway and peered out into the hallway. Miss Josephine was talking with a woman I did not know. She looked familiar, though. They were talking about showing us a demonstration of prostate milking. I listened for a few more seconds but barely heard any of the words.

I was looking hard at Miss Josephine's colleague. Simply from her bearing, I could tell that she was a Mistress. It clicked – the woman, from the photo, Mistress Beryl! Finally, the Mistress who was overseeing my training at The Haus. It all fell together in my mind. I knew what I had to do. I made a show of taking some lingerie across the hall to Miss Anita's room, walking lightly, demurely, holding the lingerie with care, looking at the floor. I felt their eyes on me and kept myself from looking their way. I did this twice more, once for Miss Serenity, once for Miss Josephine herself. On the last trip back to the laundry room, Mistress Beryl called my name. I think it was at that point that it was the most difficult to hide my smile. My intuition was strong.

Mistress Beryl called me over. I went and made her the obeisance that is her due from a Girl. She took me by the chin and looked me over as Empress Lara did. I seemed to meet with her approval. She gave me a kiss on the forehead, an honor I did not expect, and said that she'd been told that I was doing well. She knew that I had been punished, but never for anything serious like disrespecting a Miss or Mistress, but for minor infractions like the crumbs on the carpet. I can't tell you how happy I was to hear that. Approval from a Mistress I hadn't even met. Others had found me good enough to give her a positive report. What came next was even better.

She was indeed going to do a demonstration on prostate milking. Mistress Beryl would preside and Miss Josephine would also be in attendance. But, she explained, it would be a good exercise for a Girl to perform the actions. I was the newest Girl, and I had been so good – being respectful and learning well and eating the other Girls' pussies well, which I'll have to put down more about later – that I could follow their directions if I liked. I said that I would love to, and was so excited to serve and learn in this way. I asked innocently which of the Worms we would demonstrate on. Mistress Beryl said they hadn't picked one yet and waved at Miss Josephine that she would choose one. Miss Josephine's gaze met mine, and I knew that I was on the right track.

The rest of the interaction passed and Mistress Beryl went on about her business. When it was me and Miss Josephine, she gave me a sly look and asked which of the Worms I wanted to abuse. I loved her even more at that moment. I could almost taste her pussy on my tongue. I looked down shyly again. I had to make another judgment, and I made it. I knew I could have just asked Miss Josephine for Three and she'd likely have given him, but I decided to give her the details. She knew that hazing happened at The Haus but when I told her what Three and the rest had done, I could see that she was disgusted. She not only agreed that I could abuse him, but gave me additional liberties.

The demonstration took place that afternoon. I thought it might have been in the medical exam room, but instead we went to the parlor. From the look of it, the parlor is the last place you'd expect to see a BDSM demonstration. Floral arrangements, throw pillows, a full high tea set. Mistress Beryl took tea with Miss Josephine and Miss Anita. We Girls were allowed to kneel on the carpet with cushions and take tea with each other. I shared a quick glance with Miss Josephine and flushed. I know that I was not being a good slave because this required an ego. But I felt almost smug as I knelt there, drinking sweet mint tea and eating crackers with hummus. I looked across the room. Three was standing in the corner facing the wall. His ass was striped red and I could see the base of a plug in his ass. The other Worms were huddled in the other corner. H poured tea into a dog bowl and took it over to them.

When us Girls finished our tea, Mistress Beryl said a word. One of the Worms put a mat down on the carpet. She motioned for me next. Three came over and stood on the mat. Two stood near us with a tray bearing supplies. I stood behind Three and waited.

Miss Josephine began to narrate. I had seen a Worm cum from pressure to his prostate before, but had never made it happen myself. Miss Josephine walked us through several positions. We began with him standing. I used a gloved finger, then two gloved fingers. He took it without complaint. I could feel his disgusting body contracting around my fingers. His little dick was half-hard already. I concentrated on what I was doing while letting Miss Josephine's words go around and through my head. Three's breathing had relaxed. I calculated when I believed he started to enjoy it, and then changed tactics. I was done being nice.

Miss Josephine pushed him down to all fours to demonstrate the doggy style position for prostate milking. I remembered that I should probably get around to finding the prostate after all as he was still only half hard and I didn't want it to take forever. It wasn't hard to find. Men are so gross. Their greatest pleasure point is a lump inside their asses. His erection immediately popped up. I rubbed his prostate hard for a little while, then eased off.

Miss Josephine ordered Three down on his back on the mat, legs up. I followed him down. The next stage of the demonstration had me using a dildo in this new position. I put some lube on it, but not nearly enough, and the toy was silicone, not glass. He groaned when I shoved it into him. I made it the most graceless, blunt penetration I could get away with. I don't know if Mistress Beryl had been told, but if she hadn't, I wasn't about to be found out. I fumbled around in his anus on purpose as if I had lost track of where the prostate was, but I was only abusing his passage because it pleased me to. And it did please me. It pleased me very much. His nasty penis was hard and lay back against his belly. He didn't need to make much noise for me to know it hurt. His hole was already very pink. From how it felt fucking him with the dildo, there was not enough lube. I'd add a bit more, but not much.

Miss Josephine lectured us about the health benefits of prostate massage, the sexual pleasure associated with it, and also noted how it could have an aspect of punishment. I couldn't help but grin. I looked at Three. His eyes were squeezed shut. I fucked his ass harder. I adjusted my grip around the base of the dildo and forced it up and down in his asshole. His eyes opened and found mine. One look communicated much. I knew he understood what was happening, and that in itself is gratifying.

I got Miss Josephine's attention and she let me whisper in her ear. At her direction, two Girls came over. Each grabbed an ankle and held Three's legs high and far apart. I spat on his hole, seated the tip of the dildo against his prostate, and began the final assault. Miss Josephine continued coolly about seminal fluid and how orgasms can be had from prostate stimulation alone but are more often produced through prostate and penile stimulation. There would be no penile stimulation for him. Tears were coming out of Three's eyes. Mistress Beryl couldn't see his face from her angle. Three's cock was against his belly, pointing downward with the curve of his back.

When Three finally came, it went exactly where I wanted it to go – from his nipples to his hair and all over his face. But, Miss Josephine said, the prostate didn't always release its complete payload with orgasm. Sometimes it needed more stimulation to get it all out. I continued fucking Three's ass until every last bit of fluid had leaked from the tip of his cock. Miss Josephine finished and beckoned the other Worms forward to clean their fellow slave up. The Girls and I washed our hands and refreshed our superiors' cups.

Mistress Beryl said that I had done well and that I could choose a reward. I felt a shock of excitement. Torturing Three had already been a reward, and now I could have another? My mind raced. What would be most pleasurable? I chose. A choice that would not only give me great pleasure but would be a strategic move for my time at The Haus. I looked at the floor and asked in my sweetest voice to eat Mistress Beryl's pussy.

Immediately I felt like I had asked too much. Had I overstepped? Was I now in terrible trouble? My fears vanished when Mistress Beryl laughed and said yes. I scrambled over to serve her. It was an even better reward than I could have thought.

That was the first time I had eaten a Mistress's pussy after Mistress Cat's. There have been others since then, and so much else, but I'm running out of space in this notebook. There will be more. I need to describe everything.

Smoking in the Girls' Room

Tuesday, 7 a.m. The air was cool and misty outside as I stepped into the Eastbank Athletic Club.

The usual members were there, practicing their Jiu Jitsu holds and throws. I let my eyes trail over them, their long, toned muscles already shining. The sounds of exertion, almost indistinguishable from sounds of pleasure, accompanied the sight of those practicing their wrestling moves. Those tight leotards clinging to sleek thighs and round asses that refused to jiggle more than a millimeter.

"Hi, Coach G!" one of the martial arts students called out, interrupting my thoughts. I smiled, waved, and headed toward the locker rooms to prepare for helping them stretch later. That was the best part of my day. I always had to wear an athletic cup to hide my inevitable erection. They could never know what was going through my head, and the pain of my cock straining against the plastic was delicious.

I know it's wrong. I know it's obscenely inappropriate. But I can't describe how it feels to run my hand down these women's long legs. The long muscles in their thighs subtly curving outward. Feeling their tendons expanding and contracting. Their chests filling with the salty air. The irresistible lift of their breasts with every inhale. No matter how snug the bra, I could see it. Their voices echoing from the high ceilings.

I know it's wrong. But it's not just the physical aspect I like. I love knowing, deep down, that my cock is rock hard under my cup and they don't know it. I put my hands all over their bodies and they let me. They have little idea of all that's going through my mind.

I want so badly to take Mrs. Martinez into the locker room. She's usually here every Tuesday, Thursday, and Friday. I know her first name, but it seems hotter to call her Mrs.

Martinez when I think of her, for some reason. She's got these amazing heavy mom tits and a plump ass. She says she's trying to get back in shape after having a baby. I think she's perfect as she is, but having a baby is insanely hard on the body, and I'm more than happy to help her on her journey to get to where she wants to be. And it also means that I have to be extra gentle and attentive with her. I don't want her to damage her abdominal muscles.

I want to lay her back and eat her pussy until she's limp and blissed out. Her fresh, clean sweat smells so good, and every so often I catch a bit of it mixed with the subtle musk of her natural body chemistry developing. Is there anything better?

There's a woman named Donna who comes here to play tennis. I don't know her but have laid eyes on her plenty of times. She's the image of a woman from an 80's workout video. A bit taller than average, a nice rack of teardrop-shaped tits, boyish hips, beach-blonde hair, and a fresh tan. I don't want to lay her back and pleasure her softly. No. Donna I would force to her knees, grab her by the hair, and facefuck her until she gagged and fought. Then I would bend her over something, pull her underwear down under her tennis skirt, and shove my cock into whichever hole it would go into first. I wanted to ruin her proud, all-American look, to cover her face with tears and smeared makeup, to make her blow-dried hair go flat.

The men's locker room was a little way down the hall from the women's. Entering the hallway, I immediately smelled something off. Something that shouldn't be there. I took another sniff. Cigarette smoke, definitely.

Another step or two revealed a woman leaning on the doorway just inside the women's space. She was tall, statuesque, with a long mane of dark hair pulled severely back. Leggings covered her long stems that went all the way up, down, and up again. A sports bra compacted her small breasts, creating firm cleavage. Tight abdominal muscles were bare to my gaze. Her long, lean arms ended in elegant hands.

She leaned nonchalantly, a lit smoke in her hand. Her high cheekbones showed clearly as she pursed her lips to take another puff from her cigarette. It looked hand-rolled, I realized. That alone intrigued me. I haven't met many women who make such a study of tobacco.

I started to speak but only managed a croak. I cleared my throat. "Ma'am?" Her eyes moved leisurely over to mine. Hazel... the thought swam through my mind. "Ma'am, you can't do that in here. If you want to smoke, you need to go outside."

She only looked at me. She let those green cat eyes travel up and down my frame. I felt like I was being examined under a microscope. That was about how big I felt in that moment. In a matter of about two seconds, I had been brought down to the size of an ant in front of a mile-high goddess.

She brought the cigarette to her lips again, took a long drag, and blew it into my face. It stung my eyes, but smelled so good. I used to smoke, but hadn't done so for a long time. Normally, the smell didn't even appeal to me anymore, and it was hard to remember that I used to be unable to go for more than a few hours without smoking before I started to feel irritable. But now? It was like being half-starved for weeks and then coming around a corner and being hit full in the face with the smell of a neighborhood barbecue. My mouth juiced up.

I shook my head and blinked. She was looking at me in the face. One dark eyebrow arched, that small gesture as lethal as a bullwhip. I realized I had been staring at her mouth with mine hanging open. She lowered her hand holding the cigarette.

"Coach G, right?" she asked, flicking ash onto my shoe.

Before I could speak or even blink again, her arm flashed out, grabbed mine, and yanked me into the women's locker room.

I'm not small, but I could feel that her hand was as strong as steel pincers. In my shock, I couldn't even react as she expertly cut my feet out from under me and threw me to the floor. The breath was knocked out of my lungs as my back hit the tile.

She stood over me, backlit by the harsh lighting far above. Her shoulders were pinned back, her head high. Her hands were held at her side. The fists were not balled, but her fingers were tight and twitched a little, as if they were dying to ball themselves up and slam into my flesh. I couldn't move. I had never felt so weak in my life.

Her back always straight, she bent her knees until she straddled my chest.

"Hmph. Some coach you are," came her voice as I tried to catch my breath. "No resistance at all. Lying on the floor like a little worm."

I could see her pert nipples through her bra and felt my cock twitch. She was not heavy, but her weight was concentrated squarely on my chest. Her thighs squeezed me like you would a horse, steadily driving the breath out of my body, bit by bit.

The woman didn't stay still for long. She shuffled her knees until her crotch was squarely over my face. Her hard shins kept my upper arms against the cold floor. I opened my mouth to protest but anything I could have said was muffled by the warm firmness of her mound pressing against my nose and upper lip.

I had no choice but to inhale her scent – fresh sweat, a whiff of deodorant, but above all, the salty sweetness that made up her unique aroma. I closed my eyes and just existed for a moment. I pressed my jaw up further against her body and pulled in all the air I still could. I heard a slight humming noise. She moved against my face, just a bit, and I was in heaven.

I hadn't had the chance to put my cup on yet, and my cock, now fully hard, would be obvious. Hell, I was pretty sure that anyone looking could also see the shape of my balls. Someone once told me that they kind of expand and contract when I'm really turned on. I'd have bet anything that it was happening and fully visible.

But the smell of her sex, the creases where it met her thighs, and her round bottom was overwhelming. She wiggled her hips, grinding against my face, and I was lost. I wanted, needed, to rip her leggings open and plunge my tongue into her cunt, her ass, anywhere she wanted it. My air was running out.

"You can't do that in here?" she said in a mocking voice. "I think I'll do whatever I like in here."

A strangled moan came from my throat as I felt her reach back and trail one fingertip along the length of my cock, so hard it was almost poking through my shorts. I was in deep shit now. Panic rose in my chest. It was getting hard to breathe, and anyone could walk in at any moment. She stroked me again. I groaned more urgently underneath her. A few more seconds and she raised herself enough for me to get a breath. She stood up again, bent, and pressed a finger against my forehead.

"You stay right. There." I obeyed. There was nothing else in the world to do. I did crane my head up to look, though. She retrieved the packet of cigarettes and a box of matches – for some reason, that made her even more attractive, that she used matches instead of a lighter – and stalked back over to me. Stalked like a feral thing, strode like an empress. The woman straddled me again, standing, this time facing away. She took another drag of her cigarette. The smoke curled like copulating angels in the canned yellow lighting. Still holding her cigarette perfectly between two fingers, she peeled down her leggings – no panties underneath – and sat right down on my face.

Immediately my entire world was her cunt. Even though my mind could not keep up, my body knew its role. My chin lifted and my tongue thrust itself upward to meet her. The leggings around her ankles imprisoned me, and I wouldn't have it any other way. My tongue and lips began a dance older than humanity. I drank her up, the finest liquor on Earth.

I could smell the smoke on the air as she continued to smoke. She was right. She could do exactly as she liked in here. I sucked and licked for what might have been minutes or hours. Either way, I was in heaven. Every so often, she would reach forward and run her finger up and down my shaft. A couple times she even made light circles on my balls, and that almost made me cum in my shorts. Once, a bit of hot ash landed on my inner thigh, and I jumped. She only chuckled and tapped the underside of my balls with her fingertips, making me tense up.

The woman began to slide forward and back along my face, and added a new dimension to my world: her ass. I tongued the neat little pucker with as much fervor as I did her cunt. She rode me as if I were no more a man than her cigarette was. Just a thing for her to use for her pleasure. Without a name or identity. I gave myself up to it, to her. Existence had shrunk itself to the space of her body and the feeling of it on mine. My body shrieked for release at the same time as my mind wanted it to go on forever. Sounds mumbled on the outside. I didn't care what they were. The knowledge that someone could come in at any time no longer bothered me. It was there, a meek little thing that only just dared to speak, but in some odd way, I held myself blameless. After all, I was just a toy in the hand of a goddess. I had no other purpose but to please her.

She used me as long as she wanted, and stood up. Light blazed back into my eyes. My entire soul protested the loss of her slick skin against my face. I couldn't see for several seconds, but I could hear better. I heard giggles. They rippled across the consciousness like the convolutions of my own brain.

While my eyes adjusted, I started to see other people standing around us. I heard them talking. The voices sounded familiar. I tried hard to focus. Out of all the things that had gone on that day, the next things were what I least expected. Donna. Mrs. Martinez. The lights got hazy again.

They all used my face, one after the other. Either more women came into the locker room or they used my face multiple times. I don't know and I don't really care, but I'm still curious. The scent of that good tobacco filled the air the whole time. I heard small, wet noises different from the ones their cunts, asses, and my mouth. I'm not totally sure, but I like to think that they were kissing each other.

I don't quite remember how it ended, but everything does. Someone slapped the inside of my thigh and told me to get up and clean myself off. With another scoff, she ground her cigarette out on my gym bag, burning a hole in it.

"Fucking simp," she tossed over her shoulder, and was gone. They left me on the floor in a puddle of humiliation and burning, unsatisfied arousal.

I wasn't able to move until there was no more noise in the locker room. Sensation came back to my limbs a little at a time. The floor was cold and everywhere that touched the tile felt painful and creaky. I pushed myself up to sit upright. My eyes immediately went to my crotch. My cock was still hard. I had never cum. There was a large wet spot on my shorts. I put a shaking hand on it and immediately drew it back. One second and it was too much. It hurt, but I needed relief.

There were voices in the hallway. I scrambled to my feet, grabbed my bag, and dodged out of the room, though I think someone in the hallway saw me come out anyway. Carefully, deliberately, I brought myself to orgasm in the men's room, shorts around my ankles in a stall like the worm I am. I dragged myself out to my students, some of whom had already left, annoyed and wondering where I was. I quickly had to call it off for that day, stumbling through my apologies. It's evening now and I've jerked off twice more. I'm doing my damnedest to fix every detail in my mind. I know I'll jack off to it forever.

Please remember to leave an honest review of this book on Amazon or Audible so you can let me and others know what you think.

Oh ... one last thing. If you've enjoyed these short stories and look forward to reading or listening to more be sure to sign up for my private readers' list by going to <u>www.Rile yBedwyn.com/private</u>. You'll be the first to know when the next book is out and perhaps even get a chance to receive a free copy of either the book or audiobook! Also, if you have any suggestions on topics for upcoming sassy stories you'll be able to send them to me as well. Until next time my sweet!